D1435499

The Companion to
SHAKER OF THE SPEARE
The Francis Bacon Story

The Companion to

SHAKER OF THE SPEARE

The Francis Bacon Story

Evidence and Arguments

Ross Jackson

Book Guild Publishing
Sussex, England

First published in Great Britain in 2005 by
The Book Guild Ltd
25 High Street
Lewes, East Sussex
BN7 2LU

Typesetting in Times by
Keyboard Services, Luton, Bedfordshire

Printed in Great Britain by
Antony Rowe Ltd, Chippenham, Wiltshire

A catalogue record for this book is available from the
British Library

ISBN 1 85776 946 5

CONTENTS

AUTHOR'S NOTE

This *Companion* complements my novel, *Shaker of the Speare; The Francis Bacon Story* by documenting the storyline chapter by chapter. This slightly unorthodox procedure was followed due to the controversial nature and historical importance of the story. After all, who wrote what are generally considered the greatest works of English literature is of major literary importance. The *Companion* provides those who are interested in the authenticity of the novel's storyline with the material to assist in making a personal judgement.

I made a great effort in the novel not to write a single line that can be proven false. This will surprise many because the story is not the one people are used to hearing, neither concerning Francis Bacon, nor concerning William Shakespeare. Nevertheless, the story may well be as close as we are ever likely to get to the truth of what really happened. Anyone who doubts this claim should study The *Companion* and its references carefully. There are good, logical reasons why the true story was suppressed and why many events were misinterpreted by historians.

A further reason for the publication of this *Companion* is to enable the reader to distinguish between verifiable facts and literary licence, i.e. what parts of the novel are fictionalised for the sake of literary flow, and which parts are known to be authentic. In fact, all the major events are authentic. The fictionalised parts are relatively few and are generally identified as such where they occur. Even some of the dialogue is authentic.

It should be noted that the evidence put forward here is by no means original. My task has been to sort through the enormous amount of material made available on these issues by an army of researchers and historians, and to make sense of it all.

The *Companion* is best read in conjunction with the novel, but it can be read independently by those whose main interest is to judge for themselves the validity of the events regarding Francis

Bacon's life, in particular his authorship of the Shakespeare works. Others will find interesting evidence regarding other controversial matters which differ from the generally accepted historical view. For example, concerning Bacon's role as son of Queen Elizabeth, his relationship to Robert, Earl of Essex, the events surrounding his political demise as chief minister of King James, and his roles in founding Rosicrucianism, in the colonisation of America and in the editing of the King James Bible.

Ross Jackson

FOREWORD

The debate about the authorship of the Shakespeare works has raged for almost two hundred years, and there is no sign of it letting up. The belief that the man from Stratford wrote the works has been called 'one of the greatest literary myths ever perpetrated on an unsuspecting public'. This view has long been acknowledged by an impressive list of observers, who, after studying the known facts about William Shakespeare and the works themselves, concluded that the Stratfordian could not possibly have written them. Besides many lesser-known researchers, the list includes Mark Twain, Benjamin Disraeli, Ralph Waldo Emerson, Samuel Taylor Coleridge, Henry James, Sigmund Freud, Walt Whitman, Friedrich Nietzsche, Otto von Bismarck, William Gladstone, Lord Palmerston, Lord Byron, William H. Furness, August Wilhelm von Schlegel, and the Yale Research Society.

So, who did write the most famous works of English literature? During the latter part of the twentieth century, supporters of Edward de Vere, Earl of Oxford, were the most vocal claimants of their man as the proper author. Francis Bacon was the major candidate in the nineteenth century, but his candidacy was damaged by the claims of a number of his supporters that he had left hidden codes in the Shakespeare works identifying himself as the author. However, these attempts at identifying coded language were widely ridiculed and dismissed as amateurish and unconvincing, and his supporters were called 'crackpots'. While I agree that the hidden codes evidence is unconvincing, the whole matter was unfortunate in the sense that there is adequate evidence of Bacon's authorship without reverting to such arguments. Nevertheless, the damage was done. Being a 'Baconian' became poitically incorrect, and the attention of many researchers turned towards other candidates.

Actually, the Bacon/Shakespeare authorship debate is far older than most people realise, going all the way back to 1597–1598 when both men were still in there thirties. At that time only a handful of works had been published under the William Shakespeare name, including the poems *Venus and Adonis* and *The Rape of Lucrece*, and the play *Henry IV*. Two of London's inner circle literary critics, Marston and Hall, both claimed that Francis Bacon was the concealed author of these works, writing under a pseudonym. We will return to this evidence later.

The debate between the 'Oxfordians' and the 'Stratfordians' continues to be a very hot topic to this day on the Internet and elsewhere. The Oxfordians present very convincing arguments that William Shakespeare could not have written the works, while the Stratfordians are even more convincing when they argue that Oxford certainly could not have done so. Very little ammunition has been used to challenge the 'Baconians', whose case has been more or less ignored in recent times.

I first heard of the claim that Francis Bacon was the son of Queen Elizabeth and wrote the Shakespeare works fairly recently from my wife, whose research on the Italian philosopher Giordano Bruno – who was a close friend and mentor of Bacon – turned up the information. But what really ignited my interest was a statement by Peter Dawkins at a lecture in London. Dawkins is head of the Francis Bacon Research Trust and one of the most knowledgeable living authorities on Francis Bacon. In his lecture, he made the shocking statement that not a single letter has ever been found written by the man from Stratford, who went by the name William Shakespeare, while there were volumes of surviving letters from most of the other literary personalities of the period. This lack of a single surviving letter struck me as being impossible if he had been the true author. Nevertheless, I was sceptical at first. I began to read some of the evidence out of curiosity, it being entirely outside my professional field. This had the advantage that I could look at the material without preconceived notions. I was finally forced to accept that the case was very convincing. I mention this in order to make the point that I have no stake in the matter, professional or otherwise, and thus no bias regarding the truth. For me, it is simply a fascinating story, which is not generally known, and one which is of immense literary significance.

I have told Francis Bacon's life story in the form of a plausible historical novel, based on historical facts and supporting circumstantial evidence. This *Companion* provides the evidence and the arguments that form the background for the events described in the novel, which may surprise readers familiar with the 'traditional' biographies of the main characters, in particular Francis Bacon and William Shakespeare. The novel is based on the premise that three 'surprising' aspects of Bacon's life are indeed true. These are his birth as the son of Queen Elizabeth, his status as a highly evolved spiritual master – including his founding role in Freemasonry and Rosicrucianism – and his concealed authorship of the Shakespeare works. All of these aspects have been and continue to be the subject of much debate. It is beyond the scope of this volume to go into detail on the pros and cons of this wide-ranging debate. Thousands of books have touched upon events that took place in the Elizabethan/Jacobean period, one of the most fascinating of human history, and hundreds of them are relevant to these issues. Opinions on these matters are wide and varied, even among scholars. Much of the evidence is, however, substantive and quite convincing. In the last analysis, the reader will have to make his or her own judgement.

Much of the documentation related to the authorship controversy did not become known until long after Bacon's death, some as late as the mid-twentieth century. Given the importance of many of the secrets involved to England's national security, and to the public images of the reigning monarchs of the period, Elizabeth and James, it should not come as a surprise that confidential information was suppressed. The public, including contemporary historians, had very incomplete information to work with. Furthermore, printing the truth about Bacon's birth would probably have sent the instigator to the Tower, as in fact happened with Mother Dowe.

One disturbing observation I have made while carrying out the research for this book is the surprisingly poor scholarship of many historians and biographers. Both Alfred Dodd and Nieves Mathews make the point that the mistakes, assumptions and undocumented personal opinions of the early historians have been repeated many times by later historians who failed to check the original source material, thus compounding the myths and errors. With time, suppositions have been presented as facts, lies as truths. The overall impressions left with the twenty-first-century public about both Bacon and Shakespeare are major distortions of the truth and often have little to do with historical facts.

For the sake of clarity, I have adopted the convention of referring to the man from Stratford as 'Shaksper' and references to the author of the literary works as 'Shakespeare'. I do not consider the difference in spelling significant, but it is the failure of many writers to make this distinction that often causes confusion.

It is difficult to find a contribution to the authorship debate that is not a one-sided presentation by a predisposed writer. One exception to this rule is a little-known study by the German psychiatrist Amelie Deventer von Kunow, who, at the time of her study of Bacon's life and works in the early 1900s, had never read any of the numerous works on the subject of the Shakespeare authorship. She tells how the true story was almost forced upon her from the information that unfolded before her eyes as she studied Francis Bacon's life from original documents rather than previous histories. She based her conclusions on hard evidence extracted from musty state archives in England, Spain, and Italy. She then confirmed her suspicions by comparing the motif and time of writing of each Shakespeare play with the standpoint and personality of Bacon at the time in a remarkable piece of literary research akin to detective work. Here are her own words from the foreword of her book *Francis Bacon; Last of the Tudors.*

'When I first devoted myself to the study of Francis Bacon's Life and Works, his literary and philosophical productions, and especially his letters, I did not suspect the crushing life-tragedy which was to be finally unfolded before me. But with all the greater clearness, from under the rubbish of years of false historical tradition, there then arose before me the true personality in the names: Francis Tudor Bacon, Baron Verulam, Viscount St Albans, ... Shakespeare, as one in its tremendous unity.'

An alternative possible explanation of the facts is the theory that Bacon and Shaksper collaborated. This is indeed an interesting hypothesis, especially if Shaksper was the genius that the Stratfordians claim he must have been. Collaboration could explain a number of things that genius alone cannot; things we will look at in this volume – for example, the *Northumberland Manuscript*; the *Promus*; the four names in *Love's Labour's Lost* from Anthony Bacon's passport; the many cases documented by scholars where Shakespeare used obscure sources directly from Greek, Latin and Italian writings that were not available in translation; the infallible legal expertise; the detailed knowledge of the European Courts and nobility; inside knowledge about seating arrangements at Gray's Inn; the absence of a library in Shaksper's home; the lack of mention of books or manuscripts in Shaksper's will; the close correspondence in their philosophies and language; the modifications to the plays after Shaksper's death in 1616; and much more.

However, there is one big problem with this hypothesis. How could Bacon, who always gave credit where credit was due, fail to ever mention the relationship or even the name of Shaksper even once in his writings and voluminous personal correspondence? How could this collaboration fail to be known to their contemporaries? How is it that there is not a single mention anywhere by anyone that the 'two major personages' of their time, living only a few minutes apart in a city of 200,000 people, even knew each other, let alone worked together? On balance, it seems far more likely that Bacon did it alone.

But does it matter who wrote the Shakespeare works? Yes, it does. For the richest meaning and greatest understanding of a literary work can only be experienced if we can understand the relationship with the author's earthly life – the source of inspiration. Of Will Shaksper's private life, almost nothing is known. With him as author, the works stand as if in an antiseptic vacuum, without reference to anything. But Francis Bacon was one of the towering personalities of his time, excelling as a philosopher, essayist, professor of law, judge, adviser to two monarchs, leading parliamentarian and chief minister, and is widely considered today to be the father of empirical science. If to this we add the secret of his royal birth, the loss of his only true love, his fight for recognition as heir to the throne, and the tragedy of his blood brother Robert, Earl of Essex, we come to realise that a truly epic and as yet unrecognised real life story lies behind what is arguably the greatest treasure of human literature. If the motivation for and timing of the writings is understood in this light, these great works, both the plays and the sonnets, take on an entirely new, more understandable and richer meaning. They tell the gripping story of a great man's life. The works are the story of his life.

The Shakespeare question is, however, only part of the dramatic story of Francis Bacon. An additional purpose of my telling the story is to encourage a long overdue recognition of one of the giants of human history, who has been unfairly maligned and misunderstood by many modern biographers, as wonderfully documented by Nieves Mathews. In particular, the events surrounding his fall from power have been grossly distorted, and an undeserved stain thus put on his name. Bacon was an island of integrity in a sea of corruption, and is an admirable role model for all ages, including our own. With regard to his moral rectitude, his noble character, his genius and his enormous influence on science, literature, government, philosophy and spirituality, he was one of the greatest persons ever to walk this earth. We are still feeling the effects of his life's work, and will continue to do so, for the Great Plan, which he deliberately set into motion, is still unfolding.

1

BLOODY MARY

It is well known that Elizabeth Tudor and Robert Dudley were both confined in the Tower of London in the period March 18 – May 19, 1554 in the Bell and Beauchamp Towers respectively. Bishop Gardiner of Winchester, Queen Mary's Chancellor of State, was confined in the Tower at the same time as Elizabeth and Robert Dudley. In his report on the Wyatt Rebellion, he mentions that a love affair had sprung up there between Elizabeth and Dudley.[1]

A chronicle of the Tower records that a monk had married the couple there.[2] There was apparently a 'secret way' between the Beauchamp and Bell Towers.[3] For at least a portion of her stay, Elizabeth was 'allowed the full liberty of the Tower and its grounds'.[4]

The imprisonment of Robert Dudley was also 'less strict' at this time.[5]

The diary of Edward VI mentions his close friendship with Robert Dudley, and the fact that Robert Dudley often met Princess Elizabeth in Court.[6] Dudley attended Edward VI during his last illness, and Edward presented him with estates in Rockingham, Easton, and Leicester.[7] Dudley and Elizabeth were playmates in childhood[8] and even had the same tutor.

Prince Philip of Spain appointed Dudley as his private ambassador to Queen Mary.[9]

2

THE VIRGIN QUEEN

The love relationship between Elizabeth and Dudley and their marriage are well documented in the many surviving letters of the Spanish ambassador de Quadra to King Philip, and one by the Venetian envoy Surian.[1] Ironically, de Quadra was one of those from whom it was most important to keep the secret. Nevertheless, he found out and informed his superiors. Later, when his correspondence was betrayed to the Queen, he was charged with saying that he 'had written to His Majesty (the King of Spain) that the Queen had been secretly married to Lord Robert at the Earl of Pembroke's house'. De Quadra's defence was that he had only reported 'that people were saying all over town that the wedding had taken place'.[2] The marriage was apparently common knowledge at the time, but not something anyone dared say publicly for fear of reprisal.

William Cecil's period of disfavour and frustration is also documented by de Quadra, where he writes in early September 1560: 'I met the Secretary Cecil whom I know to be in disgrace … he perceived the most manifest ruin impending over the Queen through her intimacy with Lord Robert… He said they were thinking of destroying Lord Robert's wife. They had given [out] that she was ill: but she was not ill at all.'

Mother Dowe's statement about Elizabeth's pregnancy, which sent her to her death in the Tower of London, is documented,[3] as is the despatch of the Spanish envoy on the same subject.[4]

The Dictionary of National Biography (XVI, p.114) records that Queen Elizabeth was secretly married to Robert Dudley on January 21, 1561 in the house of Lord Pembroke before a number of witnesses. It is not known exactly who the witnesses were. This same information, along with many other details, is also recorded in a pamphlet very critical of Robert Dudley (later Earl of Leicester) entitled *Leicester's Commonwealth*, published in Antwerp in 1584 by an unknown author, who was clearly privy to very confidential information about the English Court. Some writers have suggested that Francis Bacon was the author because this document was listed in one of Bacon's private files, along with two Shakespeare plays and other material he had written, which did not surface until 200 years after his death, known today as the Northumberland Manuscript. Sir William Cecil was suggested as a more likely author by Jean Overton Fuller.[5]

While the Bacons were sworn to secrecy, they and others in the know allowed the truth to slip out to careful observers in a number of ways. The addition of the 'Mr' in the registration book, which was definitely placed there by someone for a reason, was just one example. A 'Mr' before the name of a baby was contrary to all customs of registration, a signal that this was a very special baby. It was never done with any of the Bacons' other children.[6]

Another example was in the biography of Francis Bacon written by his close friend, confidant and personal physician, Dr William Rawley, also doubtless sworn to keep the secret, who writes that Francis 'was born in York House or York Place', a rather heavy hint at the truth, as no one but royalty could be born in the royal palace (York Place).[7]

In one of her letters which is preserved, Lady Anne left a strong hint, writing that Francis 'was his father's first chi..' inking out the last two letters as if she had said too much. Nicholas had several children before Francis, but applied to Dudley as father, it would have been true.[8]

In another letter to Anthony, Lady Anne revealed that Francis was a ward, and not her true son, writing, 'It is not my meaning to treat him as a ward; such a word is far from my motherly feeling for him. I mean to do him good.'[9]

In the official family genealogy of the Bacon family, Francis' name was never entered, the only formal connection to Nicholas Bacon being the words 'in York House' added to the birth registration statement by a different hand some years later.[10]

The many gifts to Dudley are reported in Dawkins.[11]

Ascham's revealing dedication to Elizabeth was not published until almost two hundred years later, in 1761, another example of how the truth was suppressed for such a long time.[12]

In the Spanish Simancas archives is a letter from Leicester asking for mediation by the Spanish Court to secure his acknowledgement by Elizabeth as Prince Consort.[13]

An example of Nicholas Bacon's jolly spirit is given by Francis Bacon's following tale in his own writings:

A malefactor mightily importuning the Judge on the Northern Circuit, Sir Nicholas Bacon, to save his life ... desired mercy on account of kindred. 'Prethee,' said my Lord the Judge, 'How came that in?' 'Why if it please your Lordship, your name is Bacon and mine is Hog, and in all ages Hog and Bacon have been so near kindred that they should not be separated.' 'Ay,' replied Judge Bacon, 'but you and I cannot be kindred except you be HANGED, for HOG is not BACON until it be well hanged.'[14]

This story was probably Bacon's inspiration for the lines in the Shakespeare play *The Merry Wives of Windsor*: 'Hing, hang, dog; HANG-HOG is latten for BACON, I warrant you.'

In the Essex genealogy register, three other children of Walter and Lettice Devereux were entered before 1572. It was only *after* the Queen gave Walter Devereux the title of Earl of Essex in 1572 that Robert's name was registered as the eldest son, and thus heir to the title Earl of Essex ahead of Lord Walter's own son, Walter, born in 1569.[15] It was normal at that time for the eldest boy, not the second eldest, to bear his father's Christian name. The case of Robert Devereux must have seemed strange to Walter Devereux's contemporaries who were not in on the secret. One contemporary, Sir Henry Wotton, commented on Robert Devereux 'the Earl had but a poor conceit* of him and preferred his second son, Walter.'[16]

In one letter to Walter Devereux, Elizabeth refers to 'previous letters, the contents whereof, assure yourself, our eyes and the fire only have been privy.'[17]

Walter Devereux's request to Burghley to take over responsibility for his eldest son and heir is an incomprehensible act unless the background is known.[18]

Mr Marsham's claim about Elizabeth having two sons by Leicester is on the record.[19]

It would seem that Elizabeth insisted on the phrase 'natural issue' rather than 'lawful issue' to protect Francis Bacon, whose legal rights would otherwise have been questionable.[20]

---

* Opinion.

The sign in the sky in November 1572 was a major supernova in the constellation of Cassiopeia, although this concept was unknown at the time. It died down after about two years but a remnant can still be seen by telescope more than 400 years after the event.

The prophecies of Paracelsus and Ovid are well known.[21, 22]

The astrological significance of the supernova event is described by Dawkins.[23]

The Elizabethan historian William Warner, who published several editions of *Albion's England* from 1586 on, was apparently aware of the existence of the unrecognised heir to the throne, but not until the posthumous edition of 1612 did he dare state in print: 'Hence Englands Heires-apparent have of Wales bin Princes, till Our Queene deceast concealed her Heire, I wot not for what skill'.[24] In modern language he is saying 'Until now, England's heirs to the throne have been Princes of Wales, until the deceased Queen Elizabeth concealed her heir, for what reason I do not know.'

3

SECRETS REVEALED

It is significant that Francis and Anthony went to Trinity College, Cambridge rather than St Benet's, which Nicholas Bacon had attended. Trinity College had been established and endowed by Elizabeth's father, Henry VIII. Leicester and the Queen had visited Trinity in 1564 when Leicester was appointed Lord High Steward of Cambridge University.

No bust was made of Anthony, only of Francis.[1]

Francis' notes on university life are taken almost verbatim from *The Advancement of Learning*.[2]

According to Lawrence Gerald, a copy of *Anatomie of the Minde* still exists in the Trinity College archives with corrections in Francis Bacon's own handwriting.[3] Smedley also supports Bacon as author of this particular volume.[4]

The theme of the Kenilworth/Woodstock entertainment was a lofty one that would dominate all of Bacon's future work under all the various masks he used, and would inspire others to follow his lead. This event signified nothing less than the launching of the English Renaissance in literature, though that fact would not be realised until it was all over many years later. And it was all started by a 14-year-old boy.

The image of lines from Laneham's *Hemetes* read by Leicester are hauntingly similar to the ones used several years later in *A Midsummer Night's Dream*, where Oberon says:

> ... Thou rememberest
> Since once I sat upon a promontary
> And heard a Mermaid on a dolphin's back ...

This similarity has led a number of scholars to remark that the author of the Shakespeare works must have been present at the

Kenilworth Revels in 1575 (Will Shaksper was a boy of eleven at the time and lived far from London and the royal Court in the remote town of Stratford).

The *Laneham Letter*, written in an entertaining dialect in tongue-in-cheek fashion in the style of an exuberant youth, was a very limited edition, only a dozen or so copies having being made at the time.[5]

George Gasgoigne translated the English text of the Revels and Devices of Kenilworth and Woodstock as requested by Leicester for Elizabeth, but in his accompanying letter to the Queen on January 1, 1576, he specifically disavowed authorship, saying (in modern English): 'I do not think my translations are in any way comparable with the original version, for if Your Highness compares my ignorance with the author's skill, or takes note of my crude phrases compared with his well-polished style, you will find my sentences as much disordered as arrows shot out of plows.'[6]

The Princelye pleasures at the Courte of Kenelwoorth was published anonymously on March 26, 1576 while the 51-year-old Gascoigne was still alive. No one came forward to make a claim of authorship. After Gascoigne's death in 1577, the whole Entertainment, including *The Tale of Hemetes the Heremyte* from Woodstock, was published anonymously in 1585 under the title *The Queenes Majesties entertainment at Woodstock*. Subsequently, it was attributed to Gascoigne in spite of his denial of authorship, and included in his collected works.[7] A complete record of both manuscripts was published much later by John Nichols.[8]

The *Laneham Letter* refers to *The Shepheardes Calender*, the first mention of this expression, which appeared four year's later under the mask of 'Immerito', and was later attributed to Edmund Spenser.[9]

My account of the Kenilworth and Woodstock Entertainments is based largely upon Dawkins.[10] It is generally agreed by historians that it was one of the most spectacular events of Elizabeth's reign.

There is some uncertainty around the issue of whether Leicester and Lady Sheffield were formally married or not. She claimed they were married in a Court case after his death, but lost the case. Leicester had denied it.[11]

Leicester's Commonwealth states that Walter Devereux, Earl Marshal of Ireland, was poisoned at the instigation of Leicester.[12]

The play *Historie of Errors*, performed by The Children of Paul's for the Queen in January 1577, was apparently the forerunner of *Comedy of Errors*, which, with a few revisions and additions, was performed at Gray's Inn some years later (1594) as part of Bacon's *Prince of the Purpoole* pageant, and later included in the 1623 *Shakespeare Folio*.[13]

We do not know exactly how Francis learned of his royal birth, nor is it critical to the story, but the time was very likely the summer of 1576, as will become clearer in the next chapter. The version given here is fictional, inspired in part by the so-called 'biliteral cipher story' claimed by Elizabeth Wells Gallup[14] and a very similar 'word cipher story' claimed by Orville W. Owens.[15] Both cipher stories are claimed by their authors to be encoded in the Bacon and Shakespeare writings, using two very different cipher systems. However, it has not been possible for other researchers to replicate their findings, not for lack of trying, but primarily because neither provides a clearly defined methodology that can be used to confirm or reject their analyses.[16] They must both be considered, until and unless others can carry out a well-documented replication, as being without merit, and probably pure inventions of the authors.

4

MARGUERITE

Francis' trip to France under the care of Sir Amyas Paulet, with a personal send-off from the Queen herself is a well-documented historical event, which must have seemed quite inexplicable to anyone not familiar with the secret background. No one else ever received such royal treatment.

Pierre Ambroise, in writing the first biography of Francis Bacon in 1631, writes 'And he saw himself destined to one day hold in his hands the helm of the Kingdom.' He adds that Francis Bacon was 'born in the purple' and 'brought up in the expectation of a great career.'[1] This is another way of saying that he was of royal birth, an heir to the throne. Purple at this time was a colour reserved for royalty, and it would have been an insult to the monarch for a subject to clothe himself in robes of purple. Ambroise also mentions that Francis wished to study different peoples, and travelled extensively for some years in Europe, including France, Italy and Spain.

La Jessé, who was a poet, close friend of Ronsard, and private secretary to the Duke of Anjou, wrote a revealing, unpublished sonnet dedicated to Francis Bacon, which was first discovered in the voluminous correspondence files of Anthony Bacon in the Lambeth Archiepiscopal Library by the Rev. Walter Begley in 1903. In free translation, he writes the following:

Therefore Bacon, if it chances that my Muse praises someone
It is not because she is eloquent or learned,
Although your Pallas has taught me better (how to speak);
It is because my lute sings the saintly glory
Or in these artless lines (naive) his image is imprinted
Or that thy virtue bright shines in my shade.[2]

The importance of this evidence, which first surfaced some 300 years after the event, is that it establishes clearly that Pallas Athena, the spear-shaker, was recognised by the French poets of the *pléiade* – in all likelihood before 1580, as Francis Bacon's muse. The 'tenth muse' Shake-Speare sonnet quoted (no. 38) shows that Pallas Athena was the muse of the author of the Shake-Speare sonnets. It is plausible that Francis chose the name 'Shake-Speare sonnets' because of the tenth muse long before he knew of the existence of a minor actor from Stratford with a similar sounding name (Shaksper). The sonnets were not published under the name of William Shakespeare, or any other name, but anonymously, simply as the 'Shake-Speare sonnets'.

The first edition of Part I of *l'Académie Françoise* was published in early 1578 in France under the mask of Pierre de la Primaudave Esceuyer, an otherwise unknown entity. Later portions appeared in 1589, 1594, 1602 and 1614. Extensive and convincing analysis and arguments for Bacon's authorship, which are too detailed to go into here, are presented by Smedley[3] and Dawkins.[4] The first complete English version, over 1,000 pages long, was published in 1618, has been called 'the world's first encyclopaedia in any language' and used the familiar Rosicrucian headpiece associated with Francis Bacon.

The painter Nicholas Hilliard inscribed on his portrait of Francis a telling Latin phrase expressing his admiration: 'Would I could paint his mind.' He also did a similar portrait of Robert Devereux for the Queen at about the same time. No one else received this most unusual royal treatment.

The spelling 'Shake-Speare' rather than 'Shake-Spear' may strike the modern reader as strange or an error. It is not. In Bacon's time there was no such thing as a spelling convention. No English dictionary existed. Spelling was not considered important. Anything was allowed. In the Shakespeare works the same word is often spelled differently even on the same page, for example 'horn' and 'horne', 'look' and 'looke' and many others in *Love's Labour's Lost, 1623 Folio*.[5]

5

THE INITIATION

There is no hard evidence for Francis Bacon's initiation into Freemasonry as described here, but subsequent facts in his life provide circumstantial evidence that this must have happened, and probably at about this time and place. The connection will become clearer in later chapters. One indication is the fact that Bacon was known to be a Freemason, as was King James VI of Scotland, later King James I of England. According to the Freemason historians Knight and Lomas, King James VI of Scotland had William Schaw, a colleague of Bacon's, reorganise the Masonic ceremonies in 1598–99.[1] This resulted in the introduction into Freemasonry of a third degree – the 'Fellowcraft' degree, which survives to this day, being an intermediate degree between the Entered Apprentice and Master Mason degrees. The new degree was designed to bring a knowledge of the 'hidden mysteries of nature and science' into the Masonic ideals, and Bacon was most likely the 'driving force', this being of course one of Bacon's primary lifetime goals. Bacon must have been initiated somewhat earlier when only two degrees existed. There were no known Masonic lodges in England prior to 1600 where he could have been initiated.

The Rosicrucian Order only appeared in the public domain some years later, building upon Masonic beliefs and ceremony and on the same principles, and even at times *the identical wording* as in Bacon's *Great Instauration*. As will be shown later, Rosicrucian symbolism clearly permeates much of his work, both under his own name – in particular *The New Atlantis*, as well as under his Shakespeare mask, in particular *The Tempest*.

The history and ceremonies of Freemasonry, the Knights Templar, and the Essenes, as reflected in this chapter, are based extensively on the recent research done by Freemasons Christopher Knight and Robert Lomas.[2]

13

There is no direct evidence of Bacon's astral trip to Mount Parnassus as described in the novel. The idea was inspired by Shake-Speare Sonnet 44 and the many spiritual dimensions of Bacon's life, including his premonition of his father's death and his utopia *The New Atlantis*. There are many examples of astral travels and out-of-body experiences described in modern spiritual and paranormal psychology literature.[3, 4, 5, 6]

6

ABANDONED

Love's Labour's Lost provides one of the strongest pieces of evidence of Bacon's authorship of the Shakespeare works. Even some traditional Shakespearean scholars reluctantly accept the evidence that Bacon must have written it, but are at a loss, of course, to explain how it happened to turn up in the *Shakespeare Folio* of 1623! Bacon's visit to the French Court in Paris and Navarre in 1576–77 is well known and documented in various communications, which survive. The most striking evidence of Bacon's authorship is found in the passport of Anthony Bacon, still available for scrutiny at the British Museum, where four gentlemen by the names of 'Biron, Dumaine, Longaville and Boyesse' signed his passport while Anthony and his train were in Navarre in the period 1583–1592. Jean Overton Fuller personally checked this for herself in the British Museum.[1] The correspondences to the characters 'Berowne, Dumane, Longavill, and Boyet' from *Love's Labour's Lost* are just too close to be coincidental. Whoever wrote *Love's Labour's Lost* must have had access to Anthony Bacon's passport. Fuller also points out a number of references in the comedy which are clearly based on known places and events of Francis Bacon's visit in 1576–77. The passport with its revealing signatures was first discovered in 1917, more than 300 years after Will Shaksper's death. Bacon may possibly have added the four French names to the story after Anthony's return in 1592 to add to the authenticity, without knowing them personally, as suggested in the novel.

Bacon's love for Marguerite is documented in *Argenis*, first published in 1621, after the death of Marguerite, and apparently written by Bacon under the mask of 'John Barclay', probably on his first trip to the Continent. A special key to the names used in this book, specifically identifying the characters representing Francis Bacon, Marguerite de Valois, and Elizabeth was published in a

15

much later edition by order of King Charles I, son of James I, and an admirer of Francis Bacon, who apparently wished the truth to be known. In this book, Bacon writes:

> While I call to mind the beauty and fortunes of Marguerite, and silently celebrated the good hap of the matchless Navarre in such a love, I began to myself to like and admire those things which I had before quietly beheld without being moved by them; for what was to be found more beautiful than Marguerite?[2, 3]

Note how Bacon's love was from a distance as he 'quietly beheld' her without making a 'move'; completely understandable behaviour for a 15-year-old bowled over by a beautiful but married 23-year-old Princess, who had a lover on the side, both husband and lover having loyal armies at their disposal.

Furthermore, the *Argenis* story tells us that Elizabeth was married to a man of eminence before she became Queen, that she had a son who was passed off as the son of another, that he travelled incognito to France, where he fell in love with Marguerite de Valois; that Elizabeth would not allow Francis to marry Marguerite unless King Henry would give Elizabeth France as dowry and sent troops to help defend England against Spain.[4]

Bacon's precognitory dream just before his father's death is mentioned in his writings.[5]

Though the *Fama* was published in Kassel many years later (1614), the youthful style and the story of the 16-year-old founder of the Rosy Cross brotherhood suggest that Bacon may have written it during his first trip to the Continent. The noted Cabbalist Paul Foster Case has done a thorough Cabbalist analysis of the *Fama* and the later *Confessio*, leaving no doubt about the intentions and Cabbalistic background of the author, whoever it was.[6] One of the leading authorities on Rosicrucianism, Frances Yates, does not consider the possibility of Bacon as author, but notes with some surprise the many correspondences between the *Fama* and Bacon's own writings, providing additional arguments in favour of the case for Bacon without realising it.[7] We will return to this question of authorship later at the time of the actual publication of the three major Rosicrucian documents.

7

THE SUIT

Sir Nicholas Bacon's Will is well known, a copy of which is included in Dawkins.[1] Francis' treatment must have seemed unusually harsh to anyone familiar with the Bacon family who was not aware of the truth of Francis Bacon's birth. Only if Anthony should die before Francis and without a male heir would anything significant come to Francis. Ironically this turned out to be the case many years later, although it must have seemed unlikely in 1579.

Bacon's invention of the biliteral cipher was nothing less than a stroke of genius, a quantum leap forward in science. It could be said that he invented the binary number system, which four centuries later would be the foundation of modern computer science, in order to use it in a specific application. Indeed, Bacon's codes for the 24-letter alphabet of the times (i/j and u/v were interchangeable) are exactly the first 24 numbers in the binary number system with a=0, b=1, and with the formula to continue *ad infinitum* clearly described by Bacon. Mathematicians first reinvented the system independently three centuries later. While this national security information would never be recorded in any history text, it must have given English intelligence a tremendous advantage over their rivals for the next 40 years until Bacon described the biliteral cipher code in the expanded Latin version of his *Advancement of Learning* in 1623, after his retirement from public office, and it thus entered the public domain for the first time.[2]

Bacon's double-A emblem is found in *The Shepheardes Calender* at the beginning of Chapter IV. However, *Mother Hubbard's Tale* and *The Shepheardes Calender*, are in 'traditional' accounts normally attributed to Edmund Spenser, whose name appeared on the 1591 publication of both, but first some ten years after they were written. Mather Walker points out that a significant error seems to have occurred here, as Edmund Spenser was 69 years old at the time

Shepheardes Calender was written, and had never published anything before. His elderly status is suggested in a letter of recommendation to Leicester from Sir William Pelham, Lord Justice of Ireland in which he refers to Spenser as having 'long served without any consideration of recompense, and now grown into years.'

His age is documented by a picture of his tombstone in Westminster Abbey in a publication of the 'Spenser' works in 1679, giving his year of birth as 1510.

According to Mather Walker, the birth date on the tombstone was changed to '1553' in 1778, apparently to match the 'traditional' story, which was otherwise untenable. Apparently there was another 'Spenser' who is recorded as attending Cambridge at the same time as Gabriel Harvey, born in 1553 of poor parents, but of whom little is otherwise known, and the two seemed to have been mixed together into a single entity. The proposed explanation is that 'Spenser' was a mask for Bacon. It is known that the elderly Edmund Spenser worked as a clerk for Leicester before emigrating to Ireland in 1580. Certainly the content of the works suggests a much younger author, and the theme and style of these, and particularly later works attributed to 'Spenser', including his major work *The Faerie Queene* are classic Bacon/Shakespeare, as many commentators have pointed out. The well-known correspondence between 'Immerito' and Gabriel Harvey also indicates clearly that the author of *Shepheardes Calender* was a young man. Harvey calls him 'my younge Italianate Seignoir and French Monsieur.'[3]

The sonnets that were intended to persuade Elizabeth to recognise Francis include the first seventeen. Seen in this light, they fall into a very understandable and logical pattern.[4]

The letters from Francis Bacon to Lord Burghley are well known to historians, who, not aware of the background, have been puzzled by the many references to his mysterious 'rare and unaccustomed suit' and were unable to suggest an explanation, other than the rather far-fetched idea that he might have hoped for employment or position. But then why would a commoner law student be appealing to the Queen for a job?

The Two Gentlemen of Verona was performed for the Queen and duly recorded in 1584 in the official 'Accounts of the Revels at Court' under the name *The History of Felix and Philomena* with the same content but different names compared to the later version.[5]

Contemporaries reported that a production of *Hamlet* had been performed and well received in 1585/86 according to separate accounts by Nashe and Henslowe, dating it before Will Shaksper's arrival in London.[6] *Hamlet* was also performed by Leicester's Men in Antwerp in 1586.[7] Because of the early date, Stratfordians assume that this must have been a different non-Shakespeare *Hamlet* by some other author. No copies of the older version survived.

'Election' to Parliament in Elizabethan days was more a question of arrangement with the establishment than free elections in the modern sense. A word from Burghley would have been both necessary and sufficient for the unknown 20-year-old Francis Bacon to become an MP in 1581.

The Birth of Merlin was written anonymously, but bears internal evidence of the classic Bacon style. Several later Gray's Inn plays were performed and published under his name, including *The Prince of Purpoole* in 1594.[8]

Upon his return from his second European tour at the behest of the Queen, Francis' observations were apparently included in a State paper presented to the Queen entitled *Notes on the State of Christendom*.[9]

8

THE RISE OF ESSEX

Nothing is known of the first eighteen years of Will Shaksper's life, and very little thereafter. What is known is based mostly on official legal documents. There are very few references to him by contemporaries and no evidence of any letter ever written by him. There exists one letter written to him, but not delivered, requesting a loan. There is no evidence that he ever attended school. Circumstantial evidence suggests that he did not. It is quite possible that he could neither read nor write. This was the norm for commoners in the remote town of Stratford at the time, which has been described as being 'shabby, unclean, and densely illiterate'. Even among the governing leaders of Stratford, 13 out of 19 could not sign their names, but rather used a 'blot' i.e. an identifying personal mark – in Shaksper's father's case a heavy dot with a diagonal line, rather than a signature. Then a scribe would enter the person's name. The evidence of Shaksper's illiteracy includes firstly the fact that the six known specimens of his signature strongly suggest that he used a 'blot'. Furthermore, in these known cases, the name is spelled three different ways. The second indication is the fact that his father and at least one of his daughters were known to be illiterate. It is most unlikely that a literate man would not teach his own child to read and write. The known legal documents with his name on include a marriage petition, several petty debt cases involving small amounts of money, a couple of real estate deals, and his final Will.[1, 2]

The deer-poaching explanation for Shaksper's departure from Stratford is given in an introduction to the Shakespeare plays by Nicholas Rowe in 1707,[3] and the same incident is referred to in a 1659 letter from Rector Richard Davies of Sapperton.[4]

The old tradition that Shaksper was a butcher's apprentice in his younger days is traceable to John Dowdall, who toured in

Warwickshire in 1693. He testifies that the story came from the old clerk who showed him around the church. The story is supported by the antiquary John Aubrey in an independent account published before 1680.[5]

Essex's highly emotional confrontations with Elizabeth regarding Raleigh and later, Drake, described in this chapter, are well-known historical events, as is the Queen's 'below his degree' comment to Essex upon his marriage to Frances Walsingham.[6]

9

BACON MEETS SHAKSPER

Bacon's 'all knowledge to be my province' letter to Burghley has always been somewhat of a mystery to historians. Why was this young briefless commoner barrister telling the leading minister of the realm that he was giving up any civil ambition and instead vowing to devote his life to literature and philosophy? And why should the Queen's first minister care to hear such trivia, not to speak of Bacon's wish for some modest place where he could serve the Queen, unless there was some interest of the state in the matter? The letter is full of typical Baconian *double entendres*, which are clear to anyone knowing the truth of his royal birth and expectations, such as Burghley and the Queen, who could not be in the least doubt that he was dropping his suit for recognition, but which were inexplicable curiosities to historians and others. Just to mention one example, Francis reminds Burghley tongue-in-cheek that he is 'a man born under an excellent sovereign.'[1]

Venus and Adonis could not have been published in Elizabethan times without a special licence owing to its licentious character. If the unknown Will Shaksper had written it, the difficulty of obtaining such a licence would have been enormous. But in fact it was enrolled in the Stationers' Register under the special authority of Bacon's close friend and former tutor from Cambridge, none other than the Archbishop of Canterbury, Dr John Whitgift, who must have known that Bacon was the real author.[2] It is unlikely that the Archbishop of Canterbury and former master of Trinity College, Cambridge, could have known a butcher's apprentice from Stratford, let alone authorise a first publication of a controversial nature from such an unknown quantity.

The similarity in style to the Shakespeare works seen in some of the writings of Nashe, Greene, and Peele has led some Baconians (i.e. supporters of the theory that Bacon wrote the Shakespeare works) to suggest that these three and possibly others in their circle of friends were mere masks for Bacon. The premise in the novel is not so extreme, but Bacon probably edited many of their productions and added parts with his identifiable signature of style. They probably also had an influence on Bacon's productions, but it is more difficult to see where. Some scholars have claimed to see traces of Peele, Greene, and Lyle in Shakespeare.

Greene's mention of 'Shake-scene' is well-known and might be considered a fluke coincidence having nothing to do with Will Shaksper, were it not for the descriptive quotation he uses for the actor, which is a humorous twist on a line from *Henry VI, part 3*, 'O tiger's heart wrapp'd in a woman's hide'. This is the first documented reference to the name 'Shakespeare', and was written several months before the public – with the publication of *Venus and Adonis* – heard of the name some seven months after Greene's death.

There is no record of Will Shaksper as an actor (whatever the spelling) on any role list before this time, but there is evidence of his money-lending activities. The earliest documented loan from Shaksper was seven pounds to John Clayton in 1592, about the same time as Greene's usury accusation in *Groatsworth of Wit*. We know this is true because the debt was listed in the records of Cheapside in 1592 and because Shaksper sued and recovered the amount plus costs in court in 1600.[3]

Diana Price, who wrote an unbiased (i.e. taking no position on the authorship question) analysis of the historical Will Shaksper based only on hard evidence, argues that the 'Shake-scene/usury' quote in *Groatsworth of Wit*,[4] seen in the context of the whole piece, is primarily a personal attack on Will Shaksper for his usurious money-lending activities, and a warning about the money-lender to his friends. She points out that Stratfordians tend to omit any reference to usury altogether when referring to this piece.[5]

D.L. Roper provides evidence for the early dating of *The Merry Wives of Windsor* and hence for *Henry IV* (as evidenced by the Queen's Falstaff request), and also provides the information that Nashe made an unmistakable reference to *Much Ado About Nothing* already in January, 1593.[6]

10

GATHERING CLOUDS

Looked at from the vantage point of later generations, the negotiated compromise on the war subsidy would seem to be a normal result of give and take in a democratic society. But the point to be noted here is that this was an historic first. The English system of the sixteenth century was not a true democracy at all, and definitely not used to give and take between the monarch and the people. Bacon's triple subsidy speech as given in the Commons was not identical to the version in the novel, but the essence was the same. His leadership paved the way for what came to be known later as the 'loyal opposition', a hitherto unknown concept. From this time on, one could be loyal to the monarch, and at the same time beg to differ on policy. Though a blueblood Tudor by birth, Bacon was what later generations would call a left-wing reformer, and the first parliamentary 'democrat' in history. His impact on future democratic traditions was enormous.

Bacon's ideas on reform of the Code of Law, which was an integral part of his *Great Instauration* project, also had an immense impact on future legislation, even more outside England than within. In particular, the Code Napoleon can trace its roots to Bacon, according to Dixon.[1]

The plays attributed to Marlowe are noted for having the exact style and language of the Shakespeare works. For this reason, a number of Shakespearean scholars have ascribed most of the early Shakespeare writings to Marlowe, and because of the fact that it was so difficult to account for how the Stratfordian could possibly have written them himself at such an early age. They include Hazlitt, Fleay, Chalmers, Dyce, Verity, Thorndike, Jane Lee, Algernon Swinburne and others.[2]

Theobold provides 34 pages of almost identical quotations from a number of Marlowe and Shakespeare works, that left him in no

25

doubt that the same man wrote both.[3]

Mendenhall concluded that the Marlowe and Shakespeare works must have been written by the same person, using a technique based on frequency of word lengths, which he claims leaves an identifiable 'fingerprint'. The similarity of the frequency patterns of the two authors 'astonished him'.[4] If Mendenhall's conclusion is true, and if we accept the stated scholarly view that Marlowe wrote the early plays, we would seem to have an insoluble puzzle on our hands, as neither Shaksper nor Marlowe could then have been the man who wrote both works. Shaksper was admittedly too young to write the 'Marlowe' plays, and Marlowe died in 1593 before most of the Shakespeare works were written.

Some observers, known as 'Marlovians', who, like the Baconians and Oxfordians are convinced that Will Shaksper could not possibly have written the Shakespeare works, have found a rather ingenious solution to the above puzzle. They propose that Marlowe must have somehow faked his death and gone on to write the Shakespeare works, however far-fetched and undocumented such claims might be. But a much simpler explanation is at hand that does not require conspiracy theories or mental handsprings, namely that Bacon wrote them both.

Marlowe left behind no manuscripts or other evidence that he wrote the plays attributed to him. Indeed, several of the plays were first published many years after his death. (Where were the manuscripts all those years?) On the other hand, Peter Farey found a most interesting trunk of Francis Bacon's possessions among the Anthony Bacon material in Lambeth Palace. Included were a pre-publication copy of his essays dedicated to Anthony, along with a number of copies of phrases, proverbs and sayings of Bacon's similar to the contents of his *Promus*. Also in the trunk were a number of books, mostly in Latin, French, Italian and Spanish, including some related to Marlowe, background pieces on Turkish history plausibly used for *Tamburlaine* and *The Jew of Malta*, and the plays of Terence containing a quotation employed in *Doctor Faustus*.[5] This evidence is circumstantial but supports the theory that Francis Bacon wrote the Marlowe works.

In his letter to Lord Keeper Puckering, where he appealed for support *vis-à-vis* the Queen, Bacon included a very revealing, but typically ambiguous, reference to his birthright. He wrote, 'For if it please your Lordship but to call to mind from whom I am descended, and by whom, next to God, Her Majesty ... I know you will have a compunction of mind to do me any wrong.' As a senior member of the Privy Council, Puckering would, of course, know of Bacon's royal birth.[6]

The production of *A Comedy of Errors* at Gray's Inn as part of the 1594–95 Revels is the only reference to this play before it appears in the *Shakespeare Folio* of 1623. Unfortunately, not all of the original material from the Revels has survived, but there is enough to put Francis Bacon's fingerprint firmly on the production. Bacon's most thorough biographer was Spedding, who was not aware of Bacon's royal birth, and never for a moment considered the possibility that Bacon had written the Shakespeare works. After studying the text of the masque *The Prince of Purpoole*, Spedding wrote in the 19th century that the speeches of the six counsellors 'were written by Bacon and by him alone' and that 'no one who is at all familiar with his style, either of thought or expression, will for a moment doubt'.[7] The text is generally attributed to Bacon today.[8] The Revels also included a very successful masque called *The Honourable Order of The Knights of Helmet*, which included initiation rites into a secret society, recognisable to later generations of Freemasons, but unknown at the time to the public. Among the knights' recommended reading was the relatively unknown work *The French Academy* written by Bacon. There is no mention of the name Shakespeare anywhere in the material.

Almost the same metaphor of the child chasing the bird in Bacon's well-known letter to Fulke Greville is used also in Shakespeare's *Coriolanus*:

'I saw him run after a gilden butterfly; and when he caught it he let it go again, and after it again, and over and over he comes, and up again, catch'd it again...'

It must have been difficult for contemporaries who were unaware of the family relationship to understand the Queen's generosity in giving Bacon the reversion of Twickenham, the Zenwood property, and renewing his allowance.

The *Device of the Indian Prince* is a lost play, but it was apparently focused on an 'alone Queen', Philautia, and her two sons.[9] The play was credited to Bacon according to Dawkins.[10]

The image of Will Shaksper as presented in the novel is not

27

very attractive, and yet it is built upon the few historical facts known about the man. As Charles Dickens once said, 'The life of Shakespeare is a fine mystery and I tremble every day lest something should turn up.' The following quotation is taken from an article by Diana Price, author of *Shakespeare's Unorthodox Biography*, which she based only on actual documented historical evidence:

'Many of Shaksper's business records involve mercenary activities. In 1598, Shaksper was hoarding commercial quantities of grain during a famine. The 1598 Quiney-Sturley letters detail the correspondents' hopes of securing a sizeable loan from Shaksper. In 1604 Shaksper sold commercial quantities of malt to Phillip Rogers, loaned him two shillings, and then sued to recover £1–5*s*, 10*d* plus damages. In 1608, Shaksper sued John Addenbroke for a debt of £6 plus damages. Addenbroke skipped town, so Shaksper proceeded against the man who served as Addenbroke's security against default. In 1611, Shaksper and two others filed a complaint to protect their real estate interests, petitioning for compensation in the event of default by other lessees and sub-lessees. The complaint was essentially a tactic for collecting outstanding, or potentially outstanding moneys owed. In 1614, Shaksper was "conniving" over the pasture enclosures at Welcombe. As Robert Bearman has shown, Shaksper put his own interests before those of his community in the matter of the enclosures, again demonstrating his pre-occupation with protecting and increasing his estate. These records show that others viewed Shaksper as a likely source of loans, provided the terms were right. They also show him to have been a tight-fisted and shrewd businessman with a mean streak, a portrait to keep in mind when considering the charge that Shaksper was a usurer.'[11]

Can this be the same man who wrote, 'neither a borrower nor a lender be' and 'the quality of mercy is not strained'?

Rowe mentions the story of the one thousand pounds given to Shaksper by the Earl of Southampton.[12] Shortly afterwards, Shaksper, who had shown no previous signs of wealth or source of major income, purchased the 'second best house in Stratford' for sixty pounds (May 1597), purchased a ten percent interest in Burbage's new Globe Theatre for apparently 240 pounds (1599), and purchased 107 acres of land in the Stratford area for 320 pounds (1602) from John Combe.[13] There is no evidence of any services rendered or connection whatsoever between Shaksper and Southampton.

Shaksper was associated with two known usurers. The first was

Francis Langley, who, along with Shaksper, was accused of assaulting William Wayte in Southwark in 1596. Both were subjected to a peace bond. The second was his lifelong acquaintance John Combe, who made his fortune from usury and was acknowledged as the richest man in Stratford. Combe left five pounds to Shaksper, and Shaksper bequeathed his sword to Combe's nephew, Thomas.[14]

Will Shaksper was apparently a character worthy of parody by his contemporaries. The Court fool Falstaff is often said to be modelled on Shaksper the actor. Ben Jonson did a take-off on him in his play *Every Man Out of His Humour* in which Shaksper's motto, *Non sanz droicht* ('Not without right'), was parodied as 'Not without mustard'. This play was acted no later than 1599 and may even have included Will Shaksper in the cast as Sogliardo, the country bumpkin who tries to buy a coat-of-arms. Ben Jonson mentions later in his writings that he used Shaksper in two of his plays, including this one.

In *The Return from Parnassus*, a Cambridge student sketch put on in 1601, when making fun of contemporary actors, two lines seem clearly addressed to Shaksper, recent purchaser of property and now a certified gentleman:

> Mouthing words that better wits have framed,
> They purchase lands, and now esquires are made.[15]

The students were, like the early Ben Jonson, clearly not in on the secret. Their reaction was much like Jonson's *Poet-Ape*, portraying Shakespeare as a country bumpkin who plagiarised others' ideas. Stratfordians would use this as an indication that Shaksper was recognised as a playwright. However, given the Baconian hypothesis, there must have been some people who were fooled. It is interesting that those who were fooled, but had some personal knowledge of the actor's background, sensed that something was fundamentally wrong about the story of Shaksper as playwright, hence the plagiarism accusations from Jonson and the Cambridge students.

Was Will Shaksper an actor as well as a money-lender and investor? The evidence suggests that he was at times a minor actor, but not a particularly noteworthy one. Supporting evidence for this assessment are the detailed records kept by Edward Alleyn, one of the leading actors of the day. Alleyn kept careful records, which were published in 1841 and 1843. Sir George Greenwood wrote that these 'contain the names of all the notable actors and play-poets of Shaksper's time, as well as of every person who helped, directly or indirectly, or who paid out money or who received money in connection with the production of the many plays at the Blackfriars Theatre, the Fortune, and other theatres. His accounts were minutely stated, and a careful perusal of the two volumes shows that there is not one mention of Will Shaksper in his list of actors, poets, and theatrical comrades.'[16] The King's Men, with whom Shaksper was associated, played frequently at Blackfriars.

The only record of payment to Will Shaksper for acting is a document showing that he performed for The Lord Chamberlain's Men along with Richard Burbage and William Kempe before the Queen in December 1594. Oxfordian author Charlton Ogburn argues that the entry in the books was fraudulent.[17] Either way, the record is almost non-existent. There is no record of Will Shaksper's name connected with any particular acting role in any play, although there are many such records for other actors of the period. In E.K. Chambers' detailed compilation of acting records for the period, Will Shaksper gets two lines, while most of the well-known actors get 2–3 *pages* of mentions, suggesting that he was at most a very minor actor.[18] The name 'William Shakespeare' is mentioned twice on role lists of the King's Men performances, and in two documents relating to the King's Men and the Globe Theatre. Was he actually present, or were these few mentions of his name tributes to an absentee minority shareholder, or an attempt to exploit the name that was on the title page of the performances? We simply do not know. What is indicated from Court and tax records is that he was in Stratford regularly, if not permanently, from May 1597 until his death, but also was present at times in London.

On Will Shaksper's grave is a little four-line ditty, which may be the only thing he actually composed. It goes like this:

> Good friend, for Jesus' sake forbear
> To dig the dust enclosed here!
> Blessed be the man that spares these stones
> And cursed be he that moves my bones.

Given the much stronger evidence for the Baconian theory, one might ask why Marlovians and Oxfordians prefer their alternative theories, rather than supporting the Baconians. Aside from the hidden codes matter, the most common reason given is the difference between the style of Bacon's scientific/philosophical writings and the Shakespeare writings. The same man could not have written in two such different styles, they say. They have a valid point and it requires a response. The counter argument is that he could indeed, and we shall look at evidence supporting the claim that he could and did in fact write in two absolutely different modes.

At a general level, the argument is that Bacon was a genius who could do things no other man could do. Ironically, Stratfordians are forced to use the same genius argument to support their claims for Will Shaksper. The difference is that we know from his contemporaries that Bacon was a genius. One of his early biographers, Mallet, noted his ability to mimic the speech and character of anyone at will, writing, 'In conversation he could assume the most differing characters, and speak the language proper to each, with a facility that was perfectly natural.'[19] Other biographers have noted that he could change his writing style at will, and note an abrupt and complete change in his writing style at a particular time in his life.[20]

Bacon also had a wonderful variety at his command in manner of writing. In this respect he was a literary chameleon. E.A. Abbott says of him, 'His style varied almost as much as his handwriting; but it was influenced more by the subject-matter than by youth or old age. Few men have shown equal versatility in adapting their language to the slightest change of circumstance and purpose. His style depended upon whether he was addressing a king, or a great nobleman, or a philosopher, or a friend; whether he was composing a state paper, magnifying the prerogative, extolling truth, discussing studies, exhorting a judge, sending a New Year's present, or sounding a trumpet to prepare the way for the kingdom of man over nature.'[21] We might add, 'or writing a play,' without any exaggeration.

It would seem that Bacon had the uncanny ability when writing to consciously decide to use either his right brain or his left brain, giving him the ability to express exactly the same thought in two completely different ways. Even in his prose writings, he has been praised for his imagery and poetry by leading poets of later periods.

'He seems to have written his Essays with the pen of Shakespeare,' wrote poet and essayist Alexander Smith.

'The philosophical writings of Bacon are suffused and saturated with Shakespeare's thought', said the poet, prophet and mystic Gerald Massey.

'He is the greatest philosopher-poet since Plato,' said the poet Percy Bysshe Shelley.

'There is an understanding manifested in the construction of Shakespeare's plays equal to that in Bacon's *Novum Organum*,' said the essayist and historian, Thomas Carlyle.

Let us now look at a few examples, based on his *Essays* (including the expanded versions published in 1612 and 1625), of how Bacon was able to express the same basic idea either in prose or in verse, usually with the same metaphor. Most of the expressed ideas were far from commonplace. Many are quite unique and not found anywhere else in the literature except in these two sources. Incidentally, it was not Bacon's intention to publish the *Essays* in 1598 because they were incomplete. However, a printer who had got hold of the *Essays* and was preparing an unauthorised edition, which Bacon was unable to stop, forced his hand.[22] The *Essays* were published for the most part after the Shakespeare works were written, and could hardly have been used as source material by anyone but Bacon himself. The opposite case, that a great philosopher would have taken material from contemporary stage plays and presented them in his own writings as titbits of wisdom is just not credible. Compare!

❁

'Be so true to thyself, as thou be not false to others.'
Bacon, *Of Wisdom for a Man's Self*

'To thine own self be true,
and it must follow, as the night the day,
Thou canst not then be false to any man.'
Shakespeare, *Hamlet*

❁

'If a man look sharply and attentively, he shall see Fortune; for though she be blind, yet she is not invisible.'
Bacon, *Of Fortune*

'Fortune is painted blind, with a muffler afore her eyes,
to signify to you that Fortune is blind.
                          Shakespeare, *Henry V*

'But even, without that, a man learneth of himself, and bringeth
his own thoughts to light, and whetteth his wits as against a
    stone.'
                          Bacon, *Of Friendship*

'Peradventure* this is not Fortune's work neither, but Nature's,
who perceiveth our natural wits too dull to reason of such
    goddesses
and hath sent this natural for our whetstone, for always the
    dullness of the fool is the whetstone of the wits.'
                          Shakespeare, *As You Like It*

'They perfect nature, and are perfected by experience'
                          Bacon, *Of Studies*

'Experience is by industry achieved,
And perfected by the swift course of time.'
Shakespeare, *Two Gentlemen of Verona*

These are just a few out of dozens of examples. We will look at
more later, including some revealing examples of identical shifts
over time in various opinions on topical issues that magically occur
almost simultaneously in Bacon's and Shakespeare's writings as
late as 1623, seven years after Will Shaksper's death.

---

* Perhaps.

11

TREACHERY

The incidents in this chapter are well-known from several surviving documents, including Bacon's own *Apologie*[1] (Defence) and the confessions of Essex, Southampton, Blount, and the other conspirators who all told the same basic self-condemning story.[2] Bacon was clearly misled by Essex, but nevertheless did everything in his power to help him in spite of Essex's treachery.

In his *Apologie*, Bacon noted his premonition at the time of Essex's departure for Ireland, 'I did as plainly see his overthrow, chained as it were by destiny to that journey, as it is possible for any man to ground a judgement on future contingents.'

A curiosity in *All's Well That Ends Well* supporting the Bertram/Southampton parallel is the slip the author makes (twice in fact) referring to 'Count' Bertram as 'Earl' Bertram.[3]

Bacon writes in his *Apologie* that he had the pleasure of entertaining the Queen at Twickenham Park in the autumn of 1599, at which time he 'prepared a sonnet directly tending and alluding to draw on Her Majesty's reconcilement to my Lord (Essex)', but he does not give us any additional information about it.[4] It would be out of character for Bacon not to have included in his private papers a copy of the one sonnet he admits to have written. But it has never been found.

The *Apologie*, which Bacon published in a small volume, offers two minor pieces of circumstantial evidence of his authorship of the Shakespeare works. Both relate to the Hayward matter. Referring specifically to Hayward's book on the Richard II uprising, Bacon describes it as 'a matter, which had some affinity with my Lord's (Essex's) cause, which *though it grew from me, went about in others' names.*'[5, 6] The second instance refers to his concerns about cross-examining Essex on the Hayward book because 'it would be said *I gave in evidence mine own tales.*'[7] These curious, thinly veiled expressions make sense only if he is referring to his authorship of *Richard II* under another's name, namely William Shakespeare.

Bacon's witty 'felony' remark that the historian John Hayward had lifted whole sentences from the works of the Roman historian Cornelius Tacitus is authentic[8] and the validity of the claim has been confirmed by later scholars.

Hayward was subsequently tried and sentenced to two years in prison for writing his booklet on the Richard II uprising. Will Shaksper, though he had done precisely the same thing in the eyes of the law, was not even arrested.[9] Why not? Because the ruling elite knew very well that Will Shaksper was not the author of *Richard II*, and that the real author, Francis Bacon, was being protected by his mother, the Queen, *in her own interest*. Hayward provides us with a powerful example of why it was so necessary for Bacon to use a pseudonym.

It is well known that Edward Coke and Francis Bacon competed for the hand of Lady Hatton, and that Essex argued Francis' case with her parents. At least one source claimed that she was pregnant before the marriage to Coke, but it is not certain. She named her daughter Frances.

A remarkable document providing further evidence of Bacon's authorship was discovered in 1867. Known as the *Northumberland Manuscript*, it is the only known document directly linking Bacon and Shakespeare, both their names appearing handwritten on the cover page of a set of transcribed Francis Bacon writings from the period 1592–1597. Several of the documents mentioned on the cover page are missing. The handwriting could be Bacon's or a scribe's, or by more than one person. The remarkable thing is that, below the list of several of Bacon's known writings, two of the Shakespeare works – *Richard II* and *Richard III* – are listed, with the name 'William Shakespeare' scribbled many times nearby in different variants along with 'by Mr Francis Bacon'. The plays themselves are missing. Careful study of the contents by Frank J. Burgoyne in 1904 has dated the material to no later than early 1597. Partial evidence for this is that a handwritten copy of Bacon's first set of essays is included. As these were published in January 1597, no one would have transcribed them later than this. The most inexplicable fact is that the name William Shakespeare did not appear on any play until 1598. In 1597 the two plays *Richard II* and *Richard III* were printed anonymously! So where did Bacon

36

get the information in January 1597 that Shakespeare's name would appear on these plays in 1598? While the evidence must be considered circumstantial, it is nonetheless entirely consistent with other Baconian evidence and strengthens the case for Bacon.[10]

Bacon researcher Robert Theobald made the following point: 'If Bacon wrote Shakespeare, the *Promus* is intelligible – if he did not, it is an insoluble riddle'.[11]

Why would a busy author write down in his personal notebook over 50 pages containing 2000 expressions unless he intended to use them? No scholar disputes that this odd document, first discovered 200 years after his death, was Bacon's personal property. The interesting point is that very few of the expressions are to be found in his prose writings; but several hundred of them appear in the Shakespeare works! They include both common and uncommon forms of greetings, and many short and catchy phrases, often with a nice point, some quite original, some not, the sort of things a writer might well note down for possible future use. According to Bacon's own page dating, they were written down in 1594–1595, well before most of the Shakespeare works were written. Particularly striking evidence in this connection is the 1599 'greatly improved' quarto publication of *Romeo and Juliet*, in which 130 new words and phrases suddenly appear, which were not in the first quarto edition of 1597, but are found in Bacon's *Promus*.[12] Of the many other examples, I have quoted just a very small number here to illustrate the correspondence, courtesy of Edward D. Johnson.[13, 14] This is another of the strong Baconian arguments.

Promus	'To drive out a nail with a nail.'
Coriolanus Act 4, Sc. 7 (1623)	'One fire drives out one fire; one nail, one nail.'
Promus	'A Fool's bolt is soon shot.'
Henry V Act 3, Sc. 7 (1623)	'A Fool's bolt is soon shot.'
Promus	'Good wine needs no bush.'
As You Like It (1623) Epilogue	'Good wine needs no bush.'

Promus	'Things done cannot be undone.'
Macbeth Act 5, Sc. 1 (1623)	'What's done cannot be undone.'
Promus	'Thought is free.'
The Tempest Act 3, Sc. 2 (1623)	'Thought is free.'
Promus	'Better coming to the ending of a feast than to the beginning of a fray.'
1 Henry IV Act 4, Sc. 2 (1598)	'The latter end of a fray and the beginning of a feast.'
Promus	'Happy man, happy dole.'
Merry Wives of Windsor Act 3, Sc. 4 (1623)	'Happy man be his dole.'
Promus	'All is well that ends well.'
All's Well That Ends Well Act 5, Sc. 1 (1623)	'All's well that ends well.'
Promus	'All is not gold that glisters.'
Merchant of Venice Act 2, Sc. 7	'All that glisters is not gold.'

An interesting tale identifying Bacon as the concealed author of the two poems, *Venus and Adonis*, and *Lucrece*, and the play, *Henry IV*, is found in the writings of two well-known satirists, Joseph Hall and John Marston in 1597–98. The information is not provided in so many words, but must be dug out by sophisticated literary analysis, which has been done by various scholars. The conclusion is not disputed by Stratfordians who have studied the writings, but their reaction is: so what if two people claimed that Bacon was the concealed author of the three works. That is not proof.

The evidence is, of course, circumstantial, but I happen to think it is very relevant because it is consistent with the other evidence in this *Companion*. Two people in the heart of the London literary scene both told the world in no uncertain terms that Bacon was the real author of these works. And this was at a time when these were the only works published in William Shakespeare's name. It is especially interesting because Marston was not only a lawyer from Cambridge, and therefore very likely knew Bacon personally, but he was also a close friend of Thomas Greene, who in turn was a cousin of Will Shaksper, came from the same area, rented rooms from him at one time, and even named his children after Will and his wife Anne. So Marston was one of the few people with close links to both Shaksper and Bacon. This suggests why he knew and adds a good deal of credibility to the story. It is also relevant that Bacon's good friend and former tutor, John Whitgift, at this time Archbishop of Canterbury, ordered Hall's and Marston's satires to be burned, probably to protect Francis Bacon from unwanted publicity.[15, 16]

12

THE RING

Essex's letter to the Queen, composed by Bacon, begins, 'When the Creature entereth into account with the Creator, it can never number in how many things it needs mercy...', a thinly disguised reference to himself as her creation.[1]

Bacon's *enfants perdus* talk to the Queen, with its heavy hint of their true relationship, is paraphrased from his *Apologie*.

In a devastating critique of the 'unscholarly scholarship' of many modern historians of Bacon, Nieves Mathews documents that they have promoted a false, negative view of Francis Baccn's character with absolutely no basis in fact – a phenomenon she calls a 'character assassination'. This false view is now deeply entrenched in the public mind and so is difficult to erase. These historians prefer citing each other, and in particular the widely discredited, unscholarly writings of the nineteenth century historian Thomas Macaulay[2] rather than the less accessible but meticulously correct seven volume scholarly work of Spedding. Unlike Macaulay, Spedding based his work on actual source documents, not on private speculations. Nieves Mathews points out that later historians repeated Macaulay's flagrant errors without checking source materials, thus falsely accusing Bacon, among other things, of disloyalty and 'aggressively building the case against Essex', his patron and friend, thereby revealing a despicable personality defect. This view is quite incorrect, as pointed out by Spedding long ago (1861–1874). Yet it survives.

Bacon played no role whatsoever in 'building the case' against Essex. His role was merely to interrogate minor witnesses, an area in which he had expertise. Furthermore, under the laws of the time he could not refuse the assignment to participate in the hearing and trial on penalty of dismissal from the Queen's Learned Council and prison, because the case involved treason. Nor did his minor interventions at the trial, which were in any case designed to help

41

Essex obtain mercy, have any effect on the verdict.[3] Bacon's interventions in the Essex trial described in this chapter are a near literal copy of the actual transcript.[4]

Bacon has been a difficult man for many historians to come to terms with because he truly acted from an idealistic and spiritual – if sometimes naive – standpoint, in a time of widespread patronage and corruption. Their belief in the unlikelihood of any man acting altruistically in the real world has tempted a number of modern historians and journalists to try to tear Bacon down from his pedestal by projecting onto him, based on pure conjecture, more familiar, base motives, such as vanity, greed, self-promotion and a craving for personal power. They use a curious standard never applied to other historical figures. Without evidence, they claim that his personality must have been cold, heartless, evil, calculating, and humourless, none of which claims has a basis in any historical document, and all of which are contrary to everything said about Bacon by his contemporaries. This strange and unnerving 'character assassination' phenomenon made its first appearance after Bacon had been praised and idolised for over two hundred years, with the appearance of Macaulay's essay in 1837, and says far more about the low standard of scholarship of these latter-day historians than about Bacon. No future biographer of Bacon will be able to avoid dealing with Nieves Mathews' remarkable work unless they wish to risk repeating falsehoods about Bacon, which she has exposed once and for all.

Several historians, unaware of course of his family relationship to Elizabeth, have expressed puzzlement with Bacon's presence at Essex's trial, as he had no regular position as a law officer of the Crown. They ask themselves why a person in so subordinate a position should have been called upon when many more experienced attorneys were available. Good question – for which we now have the answer, namely to avoid an embarrassment to the Queen if the succession issue should be raised.

Elizabeth's long depression after Essex's death, and her constant murmuring of his name, are well known. This is understandable behaviour if he was her son, but not if he was a former lover, who committed treason against her, called her 'old and crooked' and was prepared to put her in prison.

Dodd gives us a number of indications that the story of the ring could be true, though we cannot be sure. Certainly only very few could possibly have known. John Webster was the first to hint at it in 1620. A second mention is an anonymous book of 1695 written by 'a lady of quality'. Bacon's biographer Montague refers to 'the last blow given by some disclosure made on the death-bed of Lady Nottingham'.[5]

The story is mentioned by historian Francis Osborne writing in 1656.[6] According to Elizabeth's biographer Strickland, the story is a tradition in the Carey family, which was very close to Queen Elizabeth.[7] A contemporary of Essex's, Camden, was of the opinion that Essex was executed because of 'obstinacy in not applying to her for mercy' by not sending the ring.[8]

Sir Walter Raleigh, when it was his turn to go to the block in 1618, confessed his sins to his friend Robert Townsend, Dean of Westminster, who accompanied him to the scaffold. He told Townsend that Essex's execution was the result of a 'trick' played on Elizabeth. The tale is recorded in a letter from Townsend to Sir John Isham, first discovered in 1930.[9]

The carving of 'Robart Tidir', the Welsh form of 'Robert Tudor', into a wooden beam in the Beauchamp Tower is a fact that has never been explained. Robert, Earl of Essex would seem to be the only person whose name might fit. If so, we have another indication of his true birthright.[10]

Bacon was commanded by the Queen to write the first draft of Essex's trial for the public record. However, it was altered and 'almost made a new writing' by his superiors against his wishes, according to Bacon's own *Apologie*, and cannot therefore be considered as his work, though his name is on it.[11]

Bacon's heated exchange with Edward Coke, although it actually took place a little later than the Essex trial, is taken almost literally from his letter to Robert Cecil, which was first made public in 1663. The actual expression Coke used for the sign on the back was *capias utlegatum* (one outside of the law). Historians agree that the letter must have been of some importance to the state but have been unable to explain why Bacon quotes a detailed personal discussion with a colleague in a letter to the Queen's first minister.

Another good question, which has now been answered. It was his duty to inform Cecil that Coke was a potential loose cannon in the matter of the succession.

13

KING JAMES

The notion that Francis deserted Essex and played a major role in bringing the guilty verdict against his 'innocent patron' would have astonished his contemporaries. This impression, which is still prevalent to this day, first surfaced some two hundred years after Bacon's death, without any supporting evidence, in the works of generally discredited historians, most notably the highly influential Macaulay, whose writings Sir Winston Churchill characterised as 'a tissue of fraud and lies'.[1]

The enormous extent of the corruption of Robert Cecil and other members of the Privy Council was first fully revealed in the 1940s when the shocking dispatches of the Spanish Ambassador Gondomar were released and published in Spain.[2] Most of the Privy Council were on Spanish retainers, and Cecil was by far the greediest. Much information of this type probably remains sealed to this day in old archives.

Historians have always been puzzled as to why Shakespeare alone among the major poets of the day failed to write a tribute to Queen Elizabeth on her death, as was the custom. Another good question that has now been answered. Bacon never got over her execution of his blood brother, Robert, Lord Essex.

The story of James' birth as the son of the Earl of Mar and Lady Mar is based on a widespread rumour, that James was substituted for the dead infant of Mary, Queen of Scots on the orders of the Queen herself. Portraits of the Earl of Mar and James VI were said to have shown an uncanny similarity of facial features. The story is supported by the finding, in 1830, of the body of an infant walled up in the royal apartments in Edinburgh Castle, where Mary is said to have given birth to the child.[3]

We do not know what sexual preferences Francis Bacon had. Some writers have claimed he was a homosexual. However, his utopian work *The New Atlantis* suggests quite the opposite. Bacon's ideal society specifically excluded 'unnatural lust' and the story relates, 'as for masculine love, they have no touch of it.'[4] Some writers have quoted occasional letters referring to his 'bedfellows', but this term had a quite different, non-sexual meaning in the 17th century as compared to our times. Due to a simple shortage of beds, it was quite common at the time to share what was available with friends of the same sex. Celibacy would seem a more likely path, given Bacon's high spiritual development, but the fact is that no one really knows. In any case, it is not important.

Bacon's remarkable letter to Cecil has been a profound mystery to historians. Why was this law professor with no public position telling the chairman of the Privy Council, Sir Robert Cecil, that 'I desire to meddle as little as I can in the King's causes,' and 'as for ambition, I do assure your honour, mine is quenched,' and 'my ambition now I shall only put upon my pen', and by the way, 'I have found an alderman's daughter, an handsome maiden, to my liking'?[5] One can easily understand the confusion of the historians not familiar with his Tudor background and his deal with King James. And yet, for Cecil, the meaning was clear as daylight, and he reacted at once. In fact, not a word was wasted by the master of the pregnant phrase, Francis Tudor Bacon, in completing his part of the deal with King James and getting the result intended almost immediately, his knighthood, which was his passport to further advancement.

Madness is a phenomenon found in many of the Shakespeare works, including *King Lear*, *Hamlet*, *Comedy of Errors*, *Twelfth Night* and *Measure for Measure*. Modern psychologists have been amazed at the accuracy of Shakespeare's descriptions. Psychologist J.C. Bucknill suggests that watching mentally afflicted persons must have been a favourite study of Shakespeare's.[6] As Bacon did when observing Lady Anne in her later years.

One of the strongest arguments against Will Shaksper as author of the Shakespeare works is the evidence put forward by a number of leading legal authorities, that whoever the author was, he must have been a very competent legal expert. This is illustrated particularly in *The Merchant of Venice* and *Measure for Measure*, but obscure legal jargon is found throughout all the plays, even the very early ones, in hundreds of examples. Lord Penzance, a leading 19th century English judge and legal authority, makes a claim which has been verified by many other legal experts, viz. that the author had a knowledge of the technicalities of law 'so perfect and intimate that he was never incorrect'; never, no matter how complicated and rare the usage. And further, he adds, 'at every turn and point at which the author required a metaphor, simile or illustration, his mind turned ever first to the law.' Many attempts have been made by Stratfordians to show that Shakespeare's legal knowledge was not perfect, that he did make errors, but every single attempt to do so has been refuted by legal experts.[7]

According to Greenwood, at least one third of all the Shakespeare metaphors are based on legal language, often very technical to a layman. Bacon is generally recognised today as one of the most competent legal experts and judges of all time. No one has ever been able to point to a single error in the thousands of cases he processed or judged in spite of an enormous effort by his detractors to reverse just one case after his political demise.

Richard Grant White, a lawyer and noted Shakespearean, points out that although the author of the Shakespeare works also shows a vast and detailed knowledge of other fields, such as psychology, botany, medicine, and seamanship, none of them approaches the exactness and infallibility of the author's legal knowledge. He says, 'Legal phrases flow from his pen as part of his vocabulary, and parcel of his thought.'

Stratfordians have countered with the supposition that Will Shaksper could have been a clerk in an attorney's office in his younger days and picked up his knowledge there and by hanging around the Courts and lawyers in London. Aside from the fact that there is not a shred of evidence to support this suggestion, it is not credible according to Lord Campbell, a former Chief Justice (1850) and later Lord Chancellor. He points out that in that case there would have to be some trace of his name as witness to legal documents; but no signatures have been found in spite of scrutiny by researchers over half a dozen shires. Nor could the knowledge exhibited in the works be picked up by observing ordinary proceedings in the Courts and reading textbooks, says another legal expert, Lord Penzance, adding, 'Nothing short of employment in some career involving constant contact with legal questions and general legal work would be requisite.'[8] Note that this criterion rules out not only Will Shaksper, but also Edward de Vere, Earl of Oxford and Christopher Marlowe as possible authors of the Shakespeare works.

In October 1604 the Solicitor Generalship became vacant, but Bacon did not apply. Francis Bacon was undoubtedly the most qualified person for the job by any standard. In fact, chief minister Lord Burghley thought so almost ten years earlier, when only Robert Cecil's intrigues prevented him from getting the position. Bacon was on good terms with King James at this time, being a member of his Learned Counsel. Some historians, unaware of his Tudor birth and potential threat to King James, try to portray Bacon as an ambitious job seeker, and are thus puzzled about why Bacon did not apply for this particular job. Unfortunately for them, his behaviour here does not fit their theory. The reason was that he knew an appointment was out of the question until he married a commoner and thus disqualified himself as a potential claimant to the throne. Subsequent events immediately following his marriage support this interpretation.

The notion that the 'youth' in the Shakespeare sonnets was the author himself in his younger days was, as far as I am aware, first put forward by Smedley. This insight allows many meanings to then fall neatly into place, especially if Francis Bacon is acknowledged as the author. Smedley, who studied Bacon's life and work for many years, writes, 'Nothing that has been written is more perfectly Baconian in style and temperament than are the Sonnets. They breathe out his hopes, his ideals, his fears, in every line. He knew how far he towered above his contemporaries, aye, and his predecessors, in intellectual power. His hopes were fixed on that day in the distant future – today – when for the first time the meshes, which he wove, behind which his life's work is obscured, are beginning to be unravelled. It was fitting that the greatest poet which the world had produced should in matchless verse do honour to the world's greatest intellect. It was a pretty conceit. Only a master mind would dare to make the attempt.'[9] One might add that, if this were indeed what he was doing, it was another good reason for publishing the verses anonymously, as the author did, simply as the 'Shake-Speare Sonnets.' Unlike many of the plays, they were not published as a work of William Shakespeare, as many people assume. William Shakespeare's name is mentioned nowhere. But Bacon's double-A emblem (one light, one dark, suggesting something concealed) is there as it was on the first editions of *Venus and Adonis* and *Lucrece*, the *King James Bible* and the quarto editions of the Shakespeare plays.

The 'concealed poet' comment in Bacon's letter to Sir John Davies is well known and has been widely quoted. This is a strong piece of evidence in favour of the Shakespeare authorship. It is difficult to imagine what it could possibly refer to otherwise, as no poetry has ever been attributed to Bacon, save the unknown sonnet to Elizabeth mentioned in his *Apologie*, and a few verses of the Psalms, which were done at a much later date. He apparently let the secret slip out here in writing due to the gravity of his situation and the need to play whatever cards he could to garner the new King's favour.

Bacon's proposal to share scientific results in *The Advancement of Learning* resulted eventually in the formation of the Royal Society in 1662 many years after his death. The founders named Bacon as their model and inspiration. The Royal Society exists to this day and has been a major factor in the development of modern science. Some modern writers condemn Bacon for inspiring the base materialism of modern society by promoting a more effective empirical science. But this is not fair, as Bacon always emphasised the glorification of God, and the spiritual elements in his works are just as important as the material benefits to Man. This spiritual aspect of Bacon's philosophy has been totally ignored in the atheistic philosophy of modern science.

Bacon's letter to Cecil on the eve of his marriage, and the three letters he wrote shortly afterwards to Cecil, the Lord Chancellor and King James, are well known and show that he had been promised the Solicitorship once he married a commoner, and that they had not kept their promise.[10] No other interpretation is plausible. Or so one should think. Why else would he refer to his birth and his recent marriage in such letters and almost demand the appointment? And get it! However, biographers who were not aware of Bacon's Tudor background have understandably been somewhat mystified by these letters. From their restricted viewpoint they have concluded that Bacon must have been an egotistical seeker after position with no sense of modesty, as he pitifully forces himself upon the three highest-ranking members of the realm seeking a job. What a tragic misunderstanding! How completely out of keeping with his true character! Their conclusions may have some logic, but are in any case far-fetched and lack credibility. A terrible wrong had been committed against Bacon. This misunderstanding is one of the main reasons for the negative view of Bacon found in the writings of many biographers.

The closing of Francis' Union speech is authentic, as is the standing ovation. In referring to this speech, Bacon biographer W. H. Dixon wrote, 'Francis Bacon began with a shower of image and illustration that at once reminds us of Shakespeare'. Another biographer, John Nichol, though he did not accept the proposition that Bacon wrote the Shakespeare works, reluctantly admitted that there was 'something startling in the like magnificence of speech' of the two men. The statesman and the poet, he wrote 'are similar in their respect for rank and dignity, in their belief in Royal Right Divine, in their contempt for the *vulgus mutable*, depreciation of the merely commercial, and exaltation of the military spirit; above all in their view of the duty of Englishmen to knit together the forces and extend the bounds of the Kingdom.'[11]

The Bacon family boar (from Novum Organum)

Nicholas Hilliard's miniature of Francis Bacon, age 18 (courtesy Peter Dawkins and the Francis Bacon Society)

The Double-A Emblem (from the *1623 Shakespeare Folio*). Variants are found in *The Shephearde's Calender, Mother Hubbard's Tale, The King James Bible of 1611, Argenis, Venus and Adonis* and several Shakespeare plays

Gorhambury House, 18th century engraving (courtesy Peter Dawkins and the Francis Bacon Society)

Peacham's Minerva Britanna, p.33
(photo Peter Dawkins, courtesy the Francis
Bacon Society)

Peacham's Minerva Britanna, p.34
(photo Peter Dawkins, courtesy the Francis
Bacon Society)

Venus and Adonis Headpiece

Shake-Speare Sonnets Headpiece

Manes Verulamiani Headpiece

Bacon's Novum Organum Headpiece, also found in the *1623 Shakespeare Folio, The King James Bible of 1611*, and *Spenser's Faerie Queen*

The Droeshout Will Shaksper from the *1623 Shakespeare Folio*

The Sunburst Face from Canonbury Tower (photo Basil Martin; courtesy The Marquis of Northampton)

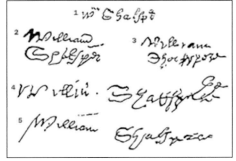

Will Shaksper signatures (sirbacon.org)

The Robart Tidir Tower of London carving (photo Lawrence Gerald of sirbacon.org)

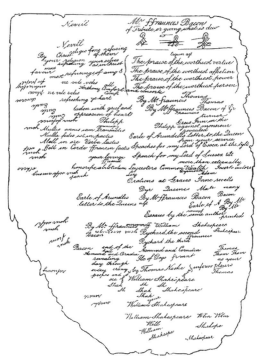

The 1910 Newfoundland Stamp
(photo Lawrence Gerald of sirbacon.org)

Facsimile of the Northumberland Manuscript
(sirbacon.org)

London 1616, from an engraving
by Claes van Wisscher

14

RISING STAR

Some interesting circumstantial evidence for the Bacon authorship is found in his correspondence at about this time with his close friend and confidant Toby Matthew, living in Europe. Bacon much appreciated Matthew's comments on his works. He was not as discreet in his correspondence with Matthew as with others. Spedding noted that much of their correspondence has been 'mutilated, erased and snipped'. Spedding also refers to Bacon's interest in Roman history at this time. Some interesting information survives in their correspondence. In one letter Francis refers directly to a previous 'model' of *Julius Caesar*, but adds, 'this which I send is more full and hath more of the narrative,' as he apparently mails an expanded version of his new play. Matthew writes back at one point in *double entendre*, 'I will not promise to return you weight for weight, but *Measure for Measure*.'[1]

Bacon reveals his Masonic background in many ways throughout the Shakespeare works. One clear example is a telling line in *Anthony and Cleopatra*, a reference that would have been understood only by Freemasons. This is an unmistakable indication of the existence of a London lodge as early as 1603, the square and rule being classic Freemason symbols.

> I have not kept my square, but that to come
> Shall all be done by the rule.*

Bacon left a subtle hint of his relationship with Elizabeth in '*In Happy Memory of Elizabeth*' when he wrote that she 'left no issue behind her, which was the case of Alexander the Great, Julius Caesar, Trajan and others'. Why, of all the comparisons he might

---

* Act II. Scene III.

have made, did he choose to name these historical leaders in particular? The reason could well be that, while none left a natural issue heir, each had a bastard or adopted son. He concluded his appraisal of Elizabeth with the comment that only with time could a final judgement be made, hinting at concealed information to be uncovered at a later date.

We have only circumstantial evidence for Bacon's role in editing the *King James Bible*. We do have evidence that Francis Bacon was invited to the 1603 Christmas festivities at Hampton Court, which included performances by the King's Men, just prior to the meeting of King James with the religious leaders to discuss and launch the Bible project.[2] But we do not know why he was invited. It seems slightly strange, as he had no position at the time. Bacon expert William T. Smedley argues the case for Bacon, referring to the set of rules, which are the only part of the Bible project that have survived, as having a 'homogeneity, breadth and vigour which point to Bacon'. He also points out that none of the classical scholars, and certainly not the two given responsibility for the final revisions for King James, Dr Miles Smith and Dr Thomas Bilson, ever published anything remotely as beautiful, before or afterwards. Nor was the King, based on his known works, capable of such a feat. It is known that the King had the draft in his possession for a full year before it was magically transformed into a work of art. Any other explanation than Francis Bacon would, according to Smedley, require a 'theory of divine inspiration for the occasion'. And by a committee no less! The King James version of the Bible has been claimed by many observers to be the most beautiful piece of writing in all the literature of the world.

Did Bacon then leave a subtle clue for astute observers to catch? Yes, he did; more than one in fact. Smedley points out that if we examine the 1612 quarto edition of the Bible we find that the design at the head of the title page of Genealogies is printed from the *identical block* used on the title pages of the first editions of Shakespeare's *Venus and Adonis* in 1593 and *Lucrece* in 1594. This block is one of Bacon's favourites, often called the sunburst face, a Masonic symbol known as 'the Sun in Splendour'.[3]

A carving of this 'veiled and feathered sunburst face' was found in the Compton Oak Room of Canonbury Tower, which was leased to Bacon from 1616 onwards, and was used as the headquarters for Freemasons and Rosicrucians according to Dawkins. Bacon received the Great Seal there upon his appointment as Lord Chancellor.

At the bottom of the same page as the sunburst face in the *King James Bible* is the classic Bacon emblem with the light/dark double-A design and the 'C' on the inside, the identical one used in *The Arte of English Poesie*, 1589, an anonymous publication which several observers have suggested was written by Bacon. A variant of the same double-A design is found on the dedication page of *Venus and Adonis*. In the 1612 octavo edition of the *King James Bible*, the exact same light A/dark A design is found on the title page of the Genealogies – the same as is used in several of the Shakespeare quartos and other publications associated with Francis Bacon, but seldom seen elsewhere.[4]

We do not know with certainty that Bacon advised King James on Jamestown and played such a central role in the colonisation of America as suggested in the novel, but the circumstantial evidence indicates that this was so, and that it was widely recognised at the time. He was certainly a member of the first council (board of directors) of the Virginia Company. William Strachey, who was aboard the *Sea Venture*, and was the first secretary of the Virginia Company in Jamestown, wrote the definitive story of the *Sea Venture* and the subsequent Jamestown tragedy.[5] Significantly, he dedicated his book to none other than Francis Bacon, whom he called 'a most noble father of the Virginian Plantation.' The first Bermudian coinage, known as hog-money, carried Bacon's family crest on one side and the picture of a ship under full sail, possibly inspired by Bacon's emblem from *The Advancement of Learning*, possibly the *Sea Venture*, on the other.

Three centuries later Francis Bacon's head appeared on the Newfoundland tercentenary stamp of 1910, with the caption 'The Guiding Spirit in Colonization Scheme', indicating how widespread his reputation was.

It is well know that many of the founding fathers of the American Declaration of Independence in 1776 were Freemasons and indebted to Bacon for their inspiration. It is said that Thomas Jefferson carried Bacon's portrait with him everywhere.[6] It would appear that the very survival of the English adventure in America, and the fact that the English language subsequently became the dominant language of North America, and later the world, was in no small part due to Francis Bacon's vision and perseverance.

Parliament's acceptance of Bacon as a sitting Member of Parliament while he was Attorney General was unprecedented and meant to be a singular exception due to his unique background and reputation. Ironically, the opposite happened. From that time onwards, the English Attorney General was always present in the House of Commons as a representative, not of the monarch, but of the State, following Bacon's example.

Most Shakespearean scholars agree that *The Tempest* was inspired by the story of the *Sea Venture* and that the author must have read Strachey's letter, due to the detailed correspondence of the language used in describing the storm and the breaking up of the ship.[7] The Stratfordians have a big problem explaining how Shaksper could possibly have had access to Strachey's letter, which contained very confidential information about the terrible state of affairs in Jamestown. It would have been disastrous for the English if the Spanish had learned how vulnerable the colony was. Clearly only the council of the Virginia Company and leading government officials would have had access to the Strachey letter, which was first published fifteen years later in 1625. Stratfordians surmise that Shaksper may have known Strachey because he had a theatrical background. Maybe. But Strachey first returned to London in the autumn of 1611 by which time *The Tempest* had already been written. It is well known that the first performance of *The Tempest* was put on for King James on November 11, 1611. Besides which, it would have been foolish for Strachey to show his written account to anyone at the time for national security reasons. This is another strong argument for Bacon's authorship.

Oxfordians have an even bigger problem than the Stratfordians explaining *The Tempest*, as their candidate had been dead for five years when the *Sea Venture* went aground. Furthermore, according to the following tale told by John Aubrey, it appears that de Vere was absent from London for most of the 1590s when – according to them – he supposedly was writing Shakespeare. It seems that the Earl of Oxford, while solemnly bowing to Queen Elizabeth, broke wind at the worst possible moment. He was so embarrassed by the incident of the fart that he decided to go abroad until it blew over. After seven years, when he felt it was safe to return, the Queen greeted him with: 'But my Lord, I had forgotten the fart.'[8]

Few of Bacon's biographers were aware of his spiritual dimension. As Rosicrucian scholar Frances Yates puts it: 'Modern students of

54

Bacon are not familiar with Rosicrucian literature, which has not been included in their studies nor recognized as a legitimate branch of history of thought or science.' One could add Hermeticism, magic, Freemasonry, the Cabbala, and Emblemata as additional topics unfamiliar to many modern Bacon biographers. And yet all of these are essential to a full understanding of Francis Bacon. Frances Yates adds: 'Yet though the name Rose Cross is not explicitly mentioned by Bacon in the *The New Atlantis*, it is abundantly clear that he knew the Rose Cross fiction and was adapting it to his own parable. *The New Atlantis* was governed by the R.C. Brothers, invisibly travelling as "merchants of light" in the outside world from their invisible college or centre, now called Salomon's House.' She points out that seventeenth century readers would immediately recognise the Rosicrucian influence in *The New Atlantis*, including the way the ' "cherubin's wings" seal the scroll brought from *The New Atlantis*, as they seal the *Fama*.' Seventeenth century author John Heydon goes even further, contending that *The New Atlantis* is 'practically the same as the Rosicrucian manifesto'.[9]

Though first published posthumously in 1627, and generally considered unfinished, *The New Atlantis* circulated among Bacon's friends as early as 1611. Bacon may have purposely withheld publication for fear of offending King James due to the political sensitivity of the Rosicrucian movement, which was associated with the Elector Palatine.

Bacon's sharp exchange with Coke upon his appointment to Attorney General is mentioned in his *Apophthegms*.

Francis Bacon was given written credit for his efforts in the planning of Princess Elizabeth's wedding entertainment of February 15 with these words: 'You that spared no time or travail in the setting forth, ordering and furnishing of this masque.'[10] Bacon was clearly chosen by the King because he was a recognised and accomplished playwright and theatre manager. He even wrote an excellent essay on the subject, *On Masques and Triumphs*. Bacon's *The Masque of Flowers* was performed on the occasion of the Favourite, Robert Carr's marriage at about the same time.

Johann Valentin Andreae, the author of *The Chemical Wedding of Christian Rosenkreutz* vehemently denied writing the *Fama* and the *Confessio*, and was in fact very critical of both. Nevertheless, some people still tend to attribute all three books to him, and even consider him the founder of Rosicrucianism, being unable to find an alternative. The styles and content are, however, as different as night and day. Rosicrucian scholars Frances Yates, Arthur Edward Waite and Paul Foster Case all express the opinion that Andreae did not write the two books. Case suggests that Andreae was simply an opportunist who capitalised on the excitement generated by the *Fama* and the *Confessio*.[11, 12, 13, 14] He appears to have published a rehash of a book he had written several years previously, giving it a Rosicrucian spin.

Dawkins points out that Bacon's contemporary Robert Burton revealed in 1621 that some of his contemporaries associated Elias the Artist and the Rosicrucian brother C.R.C. with a person who was 'the renewer of all arts and sciences, reformer of the world, and now living', a thinly veiled reference that could hardly apply to anyone but Francis Bacon.[15, 16]

If Will Shaksper truly authored the Shakespeare works, then the silence from the literary world following his death is more than just strange – it is incomprehensible. Honouring a major poet or playwright upon his demise was a time-honoured tradition. It should be obvious from the deafening silence that the literary establishment knew very well that the Stratfordian was only a front for Francis Bacon. Is there any other plausible explanation? The Shakespeare plays were very popular at the time, and Shakespeare had been praised several years earlier by critic Frances Meres in his survey of the English literary scene, where he wrote: 'As Plautus and Seneca are accounted for the best for Comedy and Tragedy among the Latins; so Shakespeare among the English is the most excellent in both Comedy and Tragedy.' He also praised the 'honey-tongued Shakespeare' for his *Venus and Adonis*, *Lucrece* and the Sonnets.[17] So where were all his 'admiring colleagues' in 1616?

Shaksper's Will offers further evidence that he was not the author of the Shakespeare works or anything else. There is no reference to any manuscripts or books; there is nothing to indicate the least literary interest. He could not have written the works without having a substantial library for reference, but none has ever been found, or even mentioned. Not a single letter in his handwriting has ever turned up. This is inconceivable if he was the true author of the works.

15

THE FALL

One of the recognised modern scholars of Bacon's philosophical and scientific works is Dr Harvey Wheeler. He points out that Bacon has been grossly misunderstood and undervalued. He feels that Bacon's analysis and research processes are still relevant today, especially his idea of bringing scientific development under the rule of law, and having its supposed benefits carefully monitored. This is an interesting observation in a world where scientists are researching human cloning, genetically modified organisms and biological weapons of destruction. Bacon would have strongly opposed the current commercialisation of science that responds to the market place but ignores real human needs and ethical considerations.

Bacon's thinking was revolutionary, and inspired many scientists of future generations, including Newton and Descartes, who would give him credit for inspiring their mechanical, reductionist worldview, which became the dominant scientific paradigm for more than three centuries, even to our time. But Bacon went even further, for he was not Newtonian in his thinking. His method was more general, encompassing even the emerging holistic worldview of twentieth century quantum mechanics in which only relationships exist and everything is connected, including both the observer and the observed, a fact first proved scientifically in the 1920s with Heisenberg's Uncertainty Principle. Bacon was not only ahead of *his* time – he was ahead of *our* time!

The 'studiously opaque' style of Bacon's scientific writings, Wheeler claims, was deliberate and for a good reason. Bacon feared that his ideas 'were so novel and their foundations so complex that ordinary readers would understand the words but not their deeper scientific meanings. He did not want the general estimation of the worth of his scientific writings to be determined by the opinions of philosophical incompetents.' The English version, first available in the 1800s, was unfortunately corrupted by incompetent translators biased by their mechanical Newtonian concept of science; they even omitted many key sections critical to the meaning, says Wheeler. Those who could read the Latin originals, like Kant, could and did understand Bacon correctly.[1]

I will illustrate with a couple of the most common misunderstandings that are now deeply entrenched. These are further examples of the aforementioned 'character assassination' of Bacon, based on unsubstantiated myths which in Nieves Mathews' words have 'thrived in the face of all evidence'.

A very common misquotation is Bacon's supposed recommendation 'to torture nature's secrets from her'. He never said or implied anything of the sort, and certainly did not use the word 'torture'. And yet the myth lives on. Dr Peter Pesic, a noted writer on the history of philosophy, points out that 'a close study of his works contradicts this claim. His treatment of the myth of Proteus depicts a heroic mutual struggle, not the torture of a slavish victim. By the "vexation" of nature Bacon meant an encounter between the scientist and nature in which both are tested and purified.'[2] Bacon, unlike Coke, the Cecils, Queen Elizabeth, King James, and almost all other top officials of the period, was opposed to torture. There are many examples where he advocated clemency and non-violence when others advocated torture and the death penalty.

A second common misreading of Bacon comes from certain twentieth century feminists, who claim 'Francis Bacon appealed to rape metaphors to persuade his audience that experimental method is a good thing'. Feminist science critics, in particular Sandra Harding, Carolyn Merchant, and Evelyn Fox Keller, claim that misogynous sexual metaphors played an important role in the rise of modern science. The writings of Francis Bacon have been singled out as an especially notable example. This latter viewpoint has been thoroughly discredited as baseless by the noted authority on sexuality, Professor Alan Soble of the University of New Orleans. He points out that the Bacon passages referred to by these writers do not remotely support their claims. By not reading him in the original, by omitting key words and sentences, and by introducing metaphors of rape and torture where there are none, they completely transform his meaning, says Soble.[3] Feminists should rather note that Bacon's defence of Lady Hatton and her daughter shows clearly that he opposed the chauvinistic attitude of people like Coke and King

James and was a staunch defender of women's rights at a time when they had almost none. Bacon courageously stood very much alone in his views.

Bacon's feminist critics might do well to contemplate his own wise words: 'What a man had rather were true he more readily believes. Therefore he rejects difficult things from impatience of research.'

The headpiece of Bacon's *Novum Organum* used another of his favourite designs, which is also found in Spenser's *The Fairie Queen*, the *King James Bible* of 1611, and the *Shakespeare Folio*, indelibly linking all these publications to Bacon.

Bacon thought that by writing his enlarged *Advancement of Learning* in Latin he would be communicating to future generations in what he expected would always be the most widely used international language. It is deeply ironic that he was wrong in this respect, as English would come to play that role – in large part due to his own efforts to improve the language and to colonise America.

The Parliamentary speeches in 1621 are not verbatim, but do reflect the essence of what was said. The story of Coke's authoring of the patent on 'Engrossing of Bills for Law Suits' for which the author, in his words, 'deserved to be hanged' is authentic, but was actually exposed some months after the trial.[4]

The meeting between King James and Francis Bacon shortly before he suddenly deserted his defence is based on the detailed description given by Bacon's young employee and confidant in Chancery, Thomas Bushell, first published 48 years after the event. Bushell's description of the meeting is completely consistent with all the known facts of the matter, and there is no reason to doubt its truth. Even the phrasing has a clear Baconian ring. According to Dodd, the same story was disclosed many years later by Bishop Hackett, who had access to Dean Williams' private papers after his death.[5] Bushell, who was also one of those testifying against his chief, probably under coercion, stated that he deeply regretted 'that so unparalleled a master should be thus brought upon the public stage for the foolish miscarriage of his own servants – whereof (with grief of heart) I confess myself to be one.' He added that the Chancellor 'in his own nature scorned the least thought of any base or ignoble act, and loathed bribery.'[6, 7]

We do not know how it came about that the King's advisors,

which would certainly have included Dean Williams, convinced the King that he had to choose between Bacon and Buckingham, as Bacon related to Bushell. The novel presents a plausible explanation based on known facts. There is, however, no documentation for the meeting between Williams, Coke, Selden and the King. But something of this sort must have occurred when it became clear that a bribery case could not be won against Bacon in spite of the three House committees working through the Easter recess trying to find evidence. There is no evidence that Bacon intended to use Finch or anyone else as defence counsel, but he may well have considered it. It would have made a lot of sense.

We do not know exactly what Buckingham said at the Privy Council meeting where Bacon was voted down, but he certainly voted against the proposal to terminate patents and must have had a determining influence on the outcome.[8]

The key to understanding the course of events leading to Bacon's 'confession' is the fact that he could not possibly have lost his case if he had defended himself, and the King realised this. Bacon was not corrupt; his 'confession' was for the gallery, an act of political suicide necessary to complete the picture desired by the King to save his favourite, the Earl of Buckingham. His fall was a political act. He was the victim of a *putsch*. In spite of a rush of appeals for reversals after his fall, not a single of Bacon's decrees was ever reversed. This is the incontrovertible proof of his innocence of bribery or corruption. The great majority of serious historians and legal experts who have studied the facts in detail all came to a similar conclusion. Some examples follow.

Dixon concluded that 'not a single fee or remonstrance traced to the Lord Chancellor himself could by any fair construction be called a bribe.'[9] Gardiner wrote, 'Bacon never knowingly sold justice.'[10] Gardiner, who, like Dixon and Spedding, did a very thorough study, concurred with Bacon's own appraisal that 'he had been the justest judge in England for the past fifty years.'[11] Hurstfield said that Bacon's decrees, 'turn out to be those which an honest and independent judge would have given had he been trying the cases on their merits alone.'[12] For Spedding – his major biographer, the sentence was 'the outcome of a popular clamour, stirred and steered toward him by his personal and political opponents.'[13] Those who persist in calling Bacon 'a corrupt judge', and they are many, are seriously misinformed and have not taken the trouble to look into the historical background.

Bacon's final words to King James, that a strike at the Chancellor would be followed by a strike at the Crown, are authentic and taken directly from his *Apologie*. His words were indeed prophetic, as the process James set in motion against Bacon eventually cost his son's life and throne several years later and terminated monarchical rule in England for a time.

16

THE FINAL CURTAIN

The statement of Francis Bacon to the House of Lords is a shorter version of his actual statement, but contains the essence of what he said.[1] On the trial itself, Gardiner called the House of Lords 'the most unfit body in existence to conduct a political trial.'[2] Legal scholar John Selden, a year after the trial, pronounced the sentence 'invalid, precisely because it had been inadequately recorded by the Court of Record which the House of Lords had now become.'[3]

After his interview with the King, Bacon left in his private notes the statement: 'I am ready to make an oblation* of myself to the King, in whose hands I am as clay to be made into a vessel of honour or dishonour. Yet with respect to the charge of bribery I am innocent.'[4]

Not all historians accept the view that the King requested Bacon to drop his defence in their famous meeting. However, Bacon's successful demand for his immediate release from the Tower and the suspension of his £40,000 fine is strong evidence that a deal had been made. Bacon's letter to Buckingham demanding – and getting – his immediate release was so confidential and sensitive a state secret that it was first published 221 years later, in 1842.[5] On a similar note, Bacon drafted a Will dated April 10, 1621 at which time he must have feared the possibility of what actually transpired. Thus he wrote, 'I bequeath my name to the next ages and foreign nations.'[6]

Further evidence for the existence of the deal is found in a surviving memorandum Bacon wrote to himself in preparation for a meeting with Buckingham on the matter of the agreement. He writes, 'Your Lordship knoweth as well as I what promises you made to me, and iterated them both by message and from your mouth, consisting of three things, the pardon of the whole sentence,

---

* sacrifice.

some help for my debts, and an annual (pension) which you Lordship ever set as £2,000 obtained and £3,000 in hope. Of these ... there is effected only the remission of the fine and the pardon now stayed.'[7]

Some of the most convincing evidence for the Bacon authorship is found in the hundreds of parallels in Bacon's own works and the Shakespeare works, not only in their general philosophies, including changes of opinion on various topics, but right down to almost exact wording at times. We have looked at a few examples in connection with the *Promus* and the *Essays*. But there are several hundred other examples, well documented by Theobald, Reed, Smedley, Mathers, Johnson, Cockburn and others.[8] Stratfordians discount these examples as 'pure coincidence'. However, a few of them occur *after* Will Shaksper's death, and cannot be explained away so nonchalantly. The *Shakespeare Folio* contains over 2,000 new lines and at least as many amendments inserted by someone after Shaksper's death in 1616.

Shakespearean scholars do not question their authenticity, i.e. they have the unique mark of Shakespeare on them. Stratfordians are forced to claim that these changes were written before 1616, were in the control of the King's Men (since Shakespeare makes no mention of them in his Will), but for some unknown reason were not included in the quarto editions published between 1616 and 1623. Unfortunately for the Stratfordians, even that far-fetched supposition fails to explain some of the changes. Let us review a few of the most interesting ones here.

Timon of Athens: This was a completely new play never seen or played or even hinted at by anyone before appearing in the *1623 Shakespeare Folio* out of nowhere. Shakespeareans have always been slightly puzzled. As far as anyone knew, Will Shaksper had never experienced anything remotely like Timon. The Stratford money-lender certainly did not go bankrupt from an excess of generosity like Timon. But Bacon did. Besides, if Shaksper wrote it, what happened to it? It was not mentioned in his Will. It is not recorded among the plays purchased by the King's Men or any other acting company. Furthermore, if one of them had it in its possession, why was it never performed; or if not usable, at least printed? That is what they always did with plays that were no longer of interest to theatregoers. There is no other plausible explanation: Bacon must have written it after his fall.

Coriolanus: This play, first printed in the *1623 Shakespeare Folio*, contains lines demonstrating the author's knowledge of the circulation of blood (Act 1, scene 1). The very words used by Shakespeare are often the same ones used by Bacon in his *History of Life and Death* and in his report on the experiments of William Harvey. But here is the clincher. The discovery of blood circulation by Harvey was first published in 1619 – three years after Will Shaksper's death! Bacon knew Harvey personally and wrote about his work.[9]

Hamlet: It is well known that Bacon held the view that the moon controlled the tides until 1616, when he reversed his position in his treatise *De Fluxu et Refluxu Maris*. In all the editions of *Hamlet* prior to Shaksper's death in 1616, the following lines showed that the author believed the lunar tides theory:

> The moist star,
> Upon whose influence Neptune's* empire stands,
> Was sick almost to doomsday with eclipse.
> (Act I, Sc. I in 1604 edition)

These lines were removed in the *1623 Shakespeare Folio*. Why? And on whose authority, we might well ask?[10]

When he published the *Advancement of Learning* in 1605, Bacon believed the widely held notion of the times that 'everything that has motion has sense' (i.e. intelligence). So did the author of *Hamlet*, who has Polonius saying, in all editions of *Hamlet* prior to the 1623 Folio:

> Sense, sure, you have,
> Else could you not have motion.
> (Act III, Sc. IV in 1604 edition)

Bacon changed his view by the time he published the enlarged Latin version of the *Advancement – De Augmentis Scientarium –* in 1623, in which he now declared the notion as untrue. The lines were simultaneously deleted from the *1623 Shakespeare Folio*. Why? On whose authority? Shaksper had been dead for seven years.[11]

King Henry IV: Judge Say is a character arrested and accused

---

*Roman god of the seas.

of various crimes and misdemeanours in this play. The *1623 Shakespeare Folio* included a number of new lines in his speech defending himself, which were not present in any earlier editions, not even the latest one from 1619. In the revised speech, we can almost hear Bacon's voice speaking to King James in the following lines, which were added by someone between 1619 and 1623:

> Justice with favour have I always done;
> Prayers and tears have moved me, gifts could never.
> When have I aught exacted at your hands,
> But to maintain the King, the realm, and you?
> Large gifts have I bestowed on learned clerks,
> Because my book preferred* me to the King.

Who added these lines after 1619? Is there any rational explanation other than Bacon as author of *King Henry IV*?[12]

Othello: The *1623 Shakespeare Folio* included 160 new lines in comparison with the 1622 quarto version, which was the only version printed after the play opened in 1610. One of the remarkable additions utilises the fact that the Bosphorus flows continuously in one direction, from East to West. Bacon, who studied this phenomenon, specifically mentions in *De Fluxu et Refluxu Maris* in 1616, that the Bosphorus tide never ebbs. He calls the two seas the Pontus and Propontis. The new lines in Othello:

> Like to the Pontic sea,
> Whose icy current and compulsive course
> Ne'er feels retiring ebb, but keeps due on
> To the Propontic and the Hellespont.
>   (Act III, Sc. IIII)

It could certainly not have been Will Shaksper who added these lines, unless he rose from the grave. Furthermore, if he wrote the lines prior to his death and not after, why were they not included the year before in the 1622 edition of *Othello*?[13]

Henry VIII: In this historic play, Lord Chancellor Wolsey suffers a fate similar to Bacon's and is forced to give up the Great Seal. Historical source material, which was easily accessible to any author,

---

* recommended.

mentions that two lords collected the seal from Wolsey, the Dukes of Norfolk and Suffolk. But in the *1623 Shakespeare Folio* – the only printed version of this play – *four* persons collect the seal. The author writes. 'Enter to Wolsey the Dukes of Norfolk and Suffolk, the Earl of Surrey, and the Lord Chamberlain.' Shaksper would have had no reason to invent a historically incorrect version. But Bacon had a good reason. His Great Seal was collected by *four* persons: the Lord Treasurer (Suffolk), the Lord Steward, the Earl of Arundel, and the Lord Chamberlain.[14] He was apparently sending us a subtle message.

Moving on to other circumstantial evidence, Henry Peacham, a close friend of Bacon's and rumoured to be a part of the Rosicrucian movement, published some very interesting material hinting strongly at Bacon's authorship of the Shakespeare works. In 1612 he published *Minerva Britanna*, a book of emblems. On page 33 (corresponding to the famous Gematria number code for 'Bacon' – 2+1+3+13+14), and on the facing page 34, specifically dedicated to Sir Francis Bacon by Peacham – just in case anyone missed the number code – we see two intriguing emblems.

On the left is seen the hand of a man, hidden from view, holding a spear in the act of shaking it. On the right, Bacon is bifurcating the biblical fiery serpent as he contemplates the spear on the left. Peacham is leaving us a hint that he knows that Shakespeare was a mask of Bacon.

But the most telling message is found in Peacham's 1622 publication *The Compleate Gentleman*. Peacham, who was well-connected in the world of literature in London, lists the greatest poets of recent times. He mentions Oxford, Buckhurst, Paget, Sidney, Dyer, Spenser and Daniel, but not the most famous of all, Shakespeare! This in spite of the fact that Shakespeare had been widely praised for *Venus and Adonis* and *Lucrece*, as well as 154 beautiful *Sonnets*, and his plays were among the most popular of the times. Why? Shakespeareans are mystified. The answer is that Peacham states specifically that he has *excluded those poets who were still alive in 1622*.[15] Thus Peacham is clearly telling the astute reader that Shakespeare was still *alive* in 1622. He knew very well that Shakespeare was just a mask for Bacon, who was at that time working on the *Shakespeare Folio* that would include new material in Shakespeare's name.

Ben Jonson followed Bacon's orders, presenting in the *Shakespeare*

Folio superficial praise of Will Shaksper, maintaining the myth as Bacon wished, while at the same time dropping many hints of the truth. This included the caricature of Shakespeare, the rather incredible story of how the plays were collected and put together by Cordell and Heminge, and not least his own ambiguous words. For example, he makes fun of the caricature, adding, 'Look not at his picture, but at his book.' Referring to the author he writes, 'He seems to shake a lance, as brandished at the eyes of ignorance.' This line is almost a summary of the life of Francis Bacon, the spear-shaker, inspired by his muse Pallas Athena and the English equivalent, St George of the Rosy Cross. But perhaps the heaviest hint of all is his praise of the author, comparing him to 'all that *insolent Greece or haughty Rome* sent forth.' In his subsequent publication *Discoveries* a few years later, he lauds Bacon to the skies as one who 'performed that in our tongue, which may be compared, or preferred, either to *insolent Greece or haughty Rome.*' Jonson's careful choice of this most unusual phrase to describe two different persons can only have had one intention, to send the message that they were one and the same – the author of the Shakespeare works and Francis Bacon.

An indication of the depth of Francis Bacon's literary talent is the fact that 400 years later, *The Shakespeare Folio* is the most quoted publication in history – ahead of number two, the *King James Bible*.

We do not know for certain that the *Folio* was financed by the brothers William Herbert, Earl of Pembroke and Philip Herbert, Earl of Montgomery, although it was the custom to dedicate a publication to the financial backer. The brothers were both personal friends of Bacon, whose reason for the dedication could also have been as a 'thank you' for their known financing of the Jamestown expedition when he was chairman of the Virginia Company.

The collection of 308 humorous anecdotes dictated by Bacon from his sickbed in one sitting was later published in his own name under the curious title *Apophthegms.** Historian Thomas Macaulay called it 'the best collection of jests in the world'.

Francis Bacon's widely praised prose history of *Henry VII* neatly fills in the only gap in the string of Shakespeare plays from *Richard III* to *Henry VIII*. If we include *Edward II*, normally attributed to

---

* Brief wise sayings.

Marlowe, and *Edward III*, an anonymous play often attributed to Shakespeare, the uninterrupted sequence goes even further back. *Henry VII* begins at the exact point where *Richard III* leaves off – on Bosworth Field after the defeat of Richard and the informal coronation of Henry VII. Shakespeare omitted only one king in the long sequence – Henry VII. Bacon wrote of only one king, Henry VII. Coincidence? Or perhaps another subtle message?

Bacon felt that man learns best when he has to work at it, when the teaching is partly open and partly concealed. This is the secret to understanding his method. He often said, 'It is the glory of God is to conceal a thing, but the glory of Man to find it out.'* His *Great Instauration* thus partly concealed the fourth part, the use of drama as a teaching tool. But he left us some hints in *De Augmentis*, where he writes of the importance of knowledge of the internal workings of the mind and the disposition of the character of men. We learn best from history, he says, not so much from reading as from drama, not by 'recording the deaths of illustrious persons' but 'much more from the entire body of history as often as such a person enters upon the stage.' Similarly he felt that 'poets and writers of history are the best doctors' regarding 'knowledge touching the affections and perturbations which are the diseases of the mind.' Referring directly to the fourth part, he specifically states that he is not talking about illustrations, but 'actual types and models, set as it were, before your eyes.' If we think about it, this is precisely what Shakespeare does. He teaches us with examples from history and diverse characters of all types and models, set before our eyes, live on the stage.[16] At a time when only a small minority of the population could read, Bacon realised that his ambitious plan to revolutionise society could only succeed if he were able to communicate with the majority. This he realised that he could only do through the theatre.

As opposed to the sound of silence following Will Shaksper's demise, Bacon's death was the occasion of a great outflow of tributes from the literary establishment, as well as from the country in general. A special publication resulted, known as *Manes Verulamiani*.[17]

The most striking aspect of the praises in this publication is their emphasis on his poetry rather than his prose or philosophical works, with many references to Apollo, Pallas Athena and the muses, a

---

*Paraphrase of Proverbs 25,2.

fact that ought to mystify anyone not familiar with the true story. The praises are clearly directed to the Shakespeare works and would certainly have been claimed as such if the Stratfordian had been the recipient:

'Thou were born of Minerva (the Roman name for Pallas Athena)'. – R.C. of Trinity College.

'He wrote stories of love more refined which still do interpret Great Bacon's Muse with a vigour choicer by far than the Nine Muses fabled in Story.' – Rector, King's College.

'None who survive him can marry so sweetly Themis the Goddess of Law to Pallas the Goddess of Wisdom.' – William Boswell.

'The King of the Muses.' – Thomas Randolph.

Others called him 'the master of fable', 'the noble day star of the muses', 'quirinus (spear-shaker)', 'the tenth muse', 'the learned Apollo', 'the leader of the great band of muses', 'Phoebus' (Apollo's) own chorister'.

In case anyone thought Bacon was only a philosopher and not also a concealed poet, two tributes let the cat out of the bag:

'The jewel most precious of letters concealed.' – R.C. of Trinity College.

'Part of thy works truly lie buried.' – Robert Ashley.

It is difficult, in the face of these clear words from those literary friends who knew him best, not to see that they knew he was the author of the Shakespeare works and were trying to tell the reader indirectly, without compromising Bacon's wish to maintain the myth. Indeed, they are *screaming* the truth at us. Look again at the tributes. Pallas Athena – the tenth muse was, by his own account in the Sonnets, Shakespeare's muse. Bacon never published a single poem in his life!

As if to cement their case, his friends arranged to put the sunburst face emblem on *Manes Verulamiani*, similar to the one used on the title page of the *Shake-Speare Sonnets*, firmly linking Bacon to the Shakespeare works.

The original manuscripts for the Shakespeare works have never been found, which has stimulated much speculation. Whatever happened to them? No one knows. Hence the strictly fictional account of Bacon's meeting with William Alexander, which may cast some light on the question. While Bacon and Sir William Alexander were undoubtedly good friends, there is no historic evidence for a cover operation to transfer the Knights Templar treasure to Nova Scotia, nor for Alexander seeking Bacon's advice on the matter. With such an obvious need for secrecy we could hardly expect to find direct evidence. There are, however, a number of elements of the story which are authentic. There are several indications that things may well have happened as described in the novel. Alexander was a senior Scottish Freemason and did get the Nova Scotia charter with very broad authority in 1621. There was extensive looting going on after 1615 at Rosslyn Chapel, and thus good reason for William Sinclair to be nervous and to decide to move the Knights Templar treasure. Henry Sinclair did visit Nova Scotia in 1398. The carvings in Rosslyn Chapel are authentic and are living proof of the pre-Columbus trip to America.

It is also a fact that some well-funded and very sophisticated team went to a great deal of trouble and expense to hide, with military precision, something that must be extremely valuable, on Oak Island, Nova Scotia, Canada. They used a very cleverly designed and booby-trapped underground hiding place deep in the bedrock far below the surface.

In the 1970s, wood samples retrieved from the bedrock caverns more than 200 feet below the surface were carbon-14 dated to the year 1575 +/–85 years by Goechron Laboratories of Cambridge. Underwater cameras identified what looked like chests in flooded caverns in the bedrock. To discourage unwelcome guests the deep hole was built with eleven layers of thick oak beams every 10 feet to about 126 feet, followed by an iron barrier, before hitting bedrock. Two very devilish man-made flood tunnels at 110 feet and 154 feet sloping upwards to two different beaches ensured that anyone trying to take the direct route down would be flooded, which is precisely what has happened repeatedly. In spite of attempts by several digging teams over a period of 200 years, some using professional mining engineers and the most modern equipment – as late as the 1990s – the design has to date confounded every attempt to recover the buried treasure. Drilling has brought up from the treasure chests small specimens of metal, a piece of a parchment with letters apparently inked by a quill pen, and traces of mercury. Several empty bottles with traces of mercury have been found on the surface area near the pit. A number of Masonic symbols have been found around the island; also some apparently coded messages using strange symbols. For some reason all of the many teams that have attempted to recover the treasure seem to have strong connections to the Masonic community, suggesting that the Freemasons know what is there but have lost the access key.[18, 19]

Francis Bacon suggested the use of mercury to preserve parchments in *Sylva Sylvarum*. He also described how to create an artificial spring: 'Find out a hanging ground, where there is a good quick fall of rainwater. Lay a half-trough of stone, of a good length, three or four foot deep within the same ground; with one end upon the high ground and the other upon the low. Cover the trough with brakes a good thickness, and cast sand upon the top of the brakes: You shall see that after some showers are past, the lower end of the trough will run like a spring of water.'[20] This is a good description of the very professional flood tunnels discovered on Oak Island, still functioning after 400 years.

In *The Tempest* – the first play of the *Shakespeare Folio* – Bacon may have left us a clue, as Prospero says:

> I'll break my staff,
> Bury it certain fathoms in the earth,
> And deeper than did ever plummet sound
> I'll drown my book.

Are the Shakespeare manuscripts and sensitive letters of Francis Bacon among the treasure still to be recovered from Oak Island? Could the Ark of the Covenant be there as well? Was the Rosslyn Chapel vault opened up and sealed again by William Sinclair in the 1620s? Could the Templar treasure still be there? Are the manuscripts there? If so, who built the underground facility on Oak Island? We may not have to wait long for the answers to these questions. Activities are underway on both sides of the Atlantic to literally get to the bottom of both mysteries. On the other hand, the same thing was said one hundred years ago about Oak Island.

17

RETURN TO PARNASSUS

This short episode is clearly pure fiction, but is consistent with the view advocated by many spiritual masters that our consciousness survives death. To take just one example from our own age, the Christian mystic Daskalos from Cyprus described to sociology professor Kyriacos Markides how he helps with the transition at death just as Viktor did.[1] The experience of Francis in the novel is a composite of the many descriptions by hundreds of people who have had near-death experiences.[2, 3]

18

CONCLUDING COMMENTS

So what do the critics say about the evidence put forward here on the authorship question? The definitive book on the subject was written fairly recently by N.B. Cockburn, a methodical and thorough former solicitor, who spent decades studying the question in excruciating detail before publishing his findings in 1998.[1] He writes in his introduction that his aim is 'to cut a swathe through all the nonsense, to get at the points that matter both for and against the Baconian hypothesis, and to state them fairly and accurately.' He bends over backwards to give the Stratfordian arguments fair treatment. Nevertheless, after 740 pages of scholarly analysis, he convincingly refutes all the Stratfordian points and concludes that 'pretty well everything does indeed fit Bacon' as author.

Cockburn is particularly thorough and in many cases original in his analysis of parallelisms. He presents numerous examples of cases where both Bacon and Shakespeare used the same very odd words and phrases with the same odd meanings, often being the only cases in literature where they appear. Any reader who has an objective mind will be convinced by these examples. There is really no other rational explanation. Cockburn thus elegantly solves a number of language cases that 'puzzle' the Stratfordians. The problem with most Stratfordian scholars, says Cockburn, is that they have not read Bacon. If they were more familiar with his writings, the meanings would be obvious to them.

As regards the presentation of the Baconian case prior to his work, Cockburn says, 'The Baconians have been their own worst enemies. It is probably true to say that never in any field of activity has the presentation of a valid case been so bungled for so long.' Cockburn is referring to the claims by some Baconians of dubious secret codes and anagrams in the works, which made it easy for the Stratfordians to dismiss the whole question without further study.

75

Unfortunately, Cockburn's book has not received wide circulation. A few copies are still available through the Francis Bacon Society and at the Globe Theatre in London.

Aside from the Stratfordian arguments dealt with and refuted by Cockburn, the most voluminous objections to the Baconians have either been emotional outbreaks without material substance or haughty dismissal based on two areas which are not critical to the case.

One is the question of whether the author had to be a classical scholar in order to write the plays. The Stratfordians claim that it was not necessary. They claim that a genius with a good grammar school education and access to readily available translations could have done it. Baconian scholars dispute this, citing many examples where readily available translations were not enough. They claim that the author must have used original – sometimes very obscure – Greek, Latin and Italian texts. There are classical scholars on both sides of the argument. It is difficult for non-experts to make a clear judgement. I lean toward the Baconian scholars, but in any case, the issue is not critical to the argument.[2]

The second question is whether Bacon left cryptographic evidence in the Shakespeare works or elsewhere identifying himself as author. In terms of sheer volume, this is the area where the Baconians have made the greatest effort. Unfortunately, the evidence they have put forward is not convincing to a sceptical observer. Most evidence is based on looking for acrostics and other coded forms of his name. The problem is that no incontestable proof has emerged, but only questionable evidence that could be due to chance alone or else cannot be replicated by other researchers. Some observers may find the evidence persuasive, some not. In any case, it is not necessary in order to make the case for Bacon.[3, 4, 5, 6]

To illustrate the problem, let us look at an example from the Friedmans' critical book. Walter H. Begley published a number of examples of anagrams to support the Baconian viewpoint. An anagram is a rearrangement of letters in a text to give a different message. Begley mentioned the following one from *The Tempest*:

> As you from crimes would pardon'd be
> Let your indulgence set me free.

These letters could be rearranged to yield a 'remarkable' message, says Begley, namely:

Tempest of Francis Bacon, Lord Verulam
Do ye ne'r divulge me ye words.

The problem with an anagram is that it does not yield a unique solution. So with the same letters, the message could just as easily be the following, claim the Friedmans:

I wrote every line myself. Pursue no code.
E. told me Bacon's a G. D. fraud.

When the laughter dies down, we must admit that the Friedmans have a good point.[7]

From what I have learned of Bacon's sense of humour, it would not surprise me if he purposely slipped in a few acrostics like this one from *The Tempest*:

Miranda: You have often
Begun to tell me what I am, but stopped
And left me to a bootless inquisition,
CONcluding, stay: not yet.

If he did, it was, as Ben Jonson said of him, because he 'could not pass up a jest.' But if he had really wanted to leave an unambiguous message – and I find nothing in his life story suggesting that he wanted to – he would probably have used his biliteral cipher. It is doubtful that he would have used this cipher with alternative fonts as suggested by Elizabeth Gallup, because it would have been too difficult, time-consuming and unreliable to do with the primitive printing techniques of his day, and the cipher would in any case be destroyed in subsequent printings. Bacon himself points out that the cipher can be used with any binary 'either/or' type observation, not just with alternative fonts. Bacon thought long-term. If he used this particular cipher, he would probably have used a word count in a sequence of sentences (odd/even) that would survive subsequent printings. This would have been far simpler for him to do, especially in his prose writings where he would not have to compromise his poetry. I have experimented with the method using random texts, and have discovered that it is very easy to do without noticeable changes in the meaning, simply by dropping or adding a word here and there. If Bacon did this, the message is yet to be discovered.

As regards the Oxfordian arguments for their man, I find their case very weak. Their argument is mainly based on parallels between Edward de Vere's life and the plays. But as Jerome Harner points out in a thorough and quite humorous analysis of the Oxfordian arguments, the parallels are even stronger with regard to Bacon's life.[8] The Earl of Oxford was a poet, but had a style quite unlike Shakespeare's, recognised as reasonably good but hardly outstanding historically as compared to other poets. How could Oxford write mediocre poetry under his own name while writing magnificent works under another's name? And why in the world would he do such a thing? In addition, the Oxfordians have a major problem explaining events occurring after de Vere's death in 1604, in particular the making of *The Tempest* in 1611 and the thousands of new lines, including a new play, that appear for the first time in the *Shakespeare Folio* in 1623.

Then there are the Stratfordians, whose attitude tends to be very emotional. They feel almost insulted, on Will Shaksper's behalf, that the authorship question is even raised, and they abhor any serious debate with Baconians. The main thrust of their argument seems to be, 'the man's name is on the works, stupid'. To understand the resistance from the Stratfordians, it must be realised that there is much historic inertia on the side of Shakesper as author, as the issue went unchallenged for so long, and there are now a lot of academic careers and tourist attractions with an interest in maintaining that belief, however contrary the evidence may be. For about two hundred years after the publication of the works, no one expressed any particular interest in the authorship question, mainly because the Shakespeare plays were not considered in the same light as they are today. They were not recognised as masterpieces, and for long periods were not particularly popular.

It was only in the nineteenth century, when the Shakespeare works were first fully appreciated, that a few discriminating people began asking hard questions about the author. In the meantime, traditional beliefs had become well-entrenched. Many books were written about Will Shaksper, and an uncritical and unquestioning public consumed them with great interest. What the public did not notice was that these books invariably started out with the unstated but tenuous assumption that the man from Stratford wrote the works.

These biographies were not based on the known facts of Will Shaksper's life (as in Diana Price's book) but consisted mainly of speculations about how 'he must have done that', how 'he must have travelled there', how 'he must have known this person', how 'he must have been proficient in this language', and how 'he must have been the greatest genius that ever lived', with little or no hard evidence to back up the assertions. Generations were brought up to accept this myth about Will Shaksper without question. Hence the difficulty later critics have had in dislodging this widely disseminated picture of the Stratfordian, where molehills of fact are mixed with mountains of speculation.

Barring the discovery of new and convincing historical material or other indisputable proof, the reader is left with a subjective judgement on both the Tudor birth question and the Shakespeare authorship question. In making a judgement, the reader might well heed Bacon's own suggestion as to method, because in principle, this is no different from any problem of science. We make our observations, including all the circumstantial evidence, eliminate as many possibilities as we can, and see what is left. As Bacon himself put it:

> If a man will begin with certainties,
> He shall end in doubts.
> But if he will be content to begin with doubts
> He shall end in certainties.

Francis Bacon's appeal to the world in his last testament was for 'foreign nations and the next ages' to clear his name and cherish his memory. It is my hope that Francis Bacon's last wish will now be fulfilled.

19

WHATEVER HAPPENED TO?

Most of the instigators of Bacon's fall were touched by Nemesis shortly afterwards, as if an angry god had intervened.

Even while Bacon was still alive, Lady Compton lost all her influence at Court. Spurned by Bacon's successor as Lord Keeper, Dean Williams, whom she had hoped to marry, she turned to her son, who was named Duke of Buckingham in 1623, for revenge. Buckingham saw to it that Williams was removed from office in disgrace. In contrast to Bacon's decrees, many of Williams' verdicts in the Court of Chancery were reversed.

King James died in physical and mental agony, and was succeeded by his son Charles, who eventually paid the price for his father's politics when he was put to death in 1649. The monarchy was abolished and replaced by a republican regime headed by Oliver Cromwell.

The Duke of Buckingham was murdered by an aggrieved naval officer, John Felton, in 1628, to the great joy of the populace.

Lionel Cranfield, who became Lord Treasurer, was impeached and charged with bribery, robbery, and embezzlement, the attack being led by his former ally, Edward Coke. He was removed from office, sent to the Tower and fined £200,000.

John Churchill, the key witness against Bacon, who had suspended him under suspicion of taking bribes, was reinstated in his old position at Chancery. After three years of continuing his old ways, he was finally unmasked, convicted, and sent to prison for forgery and fraud.

But some of those who should have been punished for their abuse of the monopolies got off lightly. Buckingham's brother, Edward Villiers, one of the principal benefactors of the abuses, was cleared of all blame in the Lords and was subsequently the recipient of many honours. Giles Mompesson was allowed to return from abroad and resume his alehouse extortion operation. In retrospect, only two men suffered because of the monopolies scandal: Michell, who spent two years in jail, and Bacon – one, a small fish, the other, innocent.

Lady Hatton's daughter, Frances, rejected her impotent husband, Buckingham's brother, after a short marriage and became pregnant by a lover. Their son was never recognised as a legitimate heir. Lady Hatton eventually made peace with James and Buckingham.

Of all the participants, Edward Coke fared best. He went on to lead Parliament for several more years as a popular supporter of the common man, and lived to be 82.

Bacon had no children; his wife, Lady St Albans, remarried shortly after his death and continued to live at Gorhambury.

Bacon's hope that his 'confession' would lead to broad reforms was not fulfilled. One positive result was that Coke – without blushing apparently – led the passing of the Monopoly Act and the reform of Chancery, implementing most of Bacon's suggestions and even used Bacon's text as preamble. But corruption continued to flourish. Nothing had fundamentally changed, and would not change until the 19th century.[1]

---

[1] Nieves Mathews, pp. 217–225.

20

SAID ABOUT FRANCIS BACON

'The most prodigious wit that ever I knew, of my nation and of this side of the sea, is of your lordship's name, though he be known by another.' – his closest friend, Toby Matthew.

'He was a genius second only to Shakespeare.' – Prof. Richard W. Church.

'The most exquisitely constructed mind that has ever been bestowed on any of the children of men' – Thomas B. Macaulay.

'Lord Bacon was the greatest genius that England – or perhaps any other country – has ever produced.' – Alexander Pope.

'No other author can be compared with him, unless it be Shakespeare.' – Thomas Fowler.

'No one who knew him could help loving him.' – Lucy Aiken.

'The philosophical writings of Bacon are suffused and saturated with Shakespeare's thought' – Gerald Massey.

'The wisest, greatest of mankind.' – Henry Hallam.

'Next to Shakespeare, the greatest name of the Elizabethan age is that of Bacon. Undoubtedly, one of the broadest, richest, and most imperial of human intellects.' – E.P. Whipple.

'All that were good and great admired him.' – John Aubrey.

'The wisdom displayed in Shakespeare is equal in profoundness to the great Lord Bacon's *Novum Organum.*' – William Hazlitt.

'In temper, in honesty, in labour, in humility, in reverence, he was the most perfect example that the world has yet seen.' – Dean Church.

'Here is language as supreme in prose as Shakespeare's is in verse' – Will Durant.

'No man ever spake more neatly, more pressly, more weightily, or suffered less emptiness, less idleness in what he uttered. The fear of every man that heard him was lest he should make an end.' – Ben Jonson.

'That extra-ordinary genius, when it was impossible to write a history of what was known, wrote one of what it was necessary to learn.' – Denis Diderot.

'One of the most colossal of the sons of men.' – G.L. Craik.

21

SAID BY FRANCIS BACON

'I had rather believe all the fables in the legends and the Talmud and the Alcoran, than that this universal frame is without a mind.'

'Be so true to thyself, as thou be not false to others.'

'If money be not thy servant, it will be thy master.'

'Money is like muck, not good except it be spread.'

'Knowledge is power.'

'It is a strange desire to seek power and to lose liberty.'

'Laws are made to guard the rights of the people, not to feed lawyers.'

'Hope is a good breakfast, but it is a bad supper.'

'The art of acting should be made a part of the education of youth.'

'Nature, to be commanded, must be obeyed.'

REFERENCES

1. Bloody Mary

1. Amelie Deventer von Kunow, *Francis Bacon; The Last of the Tudors* (English translation, published by the Bacon Society of America, New York, 1924), p. 10, with reference to the Gardiner document 'Wyatt's Rebellion 1554' in the New Records Office. This book is referred to hereafter as vK.
2. vK, p. 10.
3. Alfred Dodd, *Francis Bacon's Personal Life-Story* (London, Rider & Company, 1986), p. 39. This book is referred to hereafter as Dodd1.
4. Dodd1, p. 39.
5. vK, p. 10.
6. vK, p. 9.
7. vK, p. 9 with reference to the New Records Office, Dictionary of National Biography.
8. Alfred Dodd, *The Marriage of Elizabeth Tudor* (London, Rider & Company, 1940), p. 26, with reference to Froude (*England*, Vol. VI, p. 220). This book is referred to hereafter as Dodd2.
9. vK, p. 10.

2. The Virgin Queen

1. Dodd2, p. 29–31.
2. Jean Overton Fuller, *Sir Francis Bacon: A Biography* (George Mann, Maidstone, UK, 1994), p. 37, who refers to her source material as being the Calendar of State Papers, Spanish, 1558–67, p. 248. This book is referred to hereafter as Fuller.
3. Dodd2, p. 37, with reference to Parker Woodward, *Tudor Problems* (London, 1909), p. 7.
4. vK, p. 12, with reference to the records of the Escorial Palace Spanish Papers.
5. vK, p. 12.
6. Dodd2, p. 41.
7. Dodd2, p. 38.
8. Dodd2, p. 40.

9. Dodd1, p. 352.
10. 8. vK, p. 12.
11. Peter Dawkins, *Dedication to the Light* (London, Francis Bacon Research Trust, 1984), p. 45. This book is hereafter referred to as Dawkins1.
12. Dawkins1, p. 51.
13. vK, p. 16.
14. Dodd1, p. 50.
15. vK, p. 15.
16. Dodd2, p. 71.
17. Dodd2, p. 71.
18. Dodd2, p. 72.
19. Fuller, p. 41.
20. Dodd1, p. 42.
21. Paracelsus, *Treatise on Metals*, ch. 1.
22. Ovid, *Metamorphoses*, X, p. 196.
23. Peter Dawkins, *Herald of the New Age* (London, Francis Bacon Research Trust, 1989). This book is referred to hereafter as Dawkins2.
24. Dawkins1.

3. Secrets Revealed

1. Dodd1, p. 68.
2. Francis Bacon, *The Advancement of Learning* (London, Henrie Tomes, 1605).
3. See www.sirbacon.org
4. William T. Smedley, *The Mystery of Francis Bacon* (1910); on-line free book at www.hiddenmysteries.com/bacon p. 59. Referred to hereafter as Smedley.
5. Dodd1, p. 76
6. Peter Dawkins, *The Great Vision* (Coventry, Francis Bacon Research Trust, 1985), and p. 122, referred to hereafter as Dawkins3.
7. Dawkins3, p. 126
8. John Nichols, *Progresses and Public Processions of Queen Elizabeth, 1788–1821.*
9. Dawkins3 p. 126.
10. Dawkins3, p. 120–127.
11. See www.elizabeth.org
12. Dawkins2, p. 72.
13. Dawkins3, p. 292.
14. Elizabeth Wells Gallup, *The Bi-literal Cipher of Sir Francis Bacon* (Detroit, Howard Publishing Co., 1910).
15. Orville W. Owen, *Sir Francis Bacon's Cipher Story* (Montana, USA, Kessinger Publishing Company, Volumes 1–5, 1893–5).
16. William F. and Elizabeth S. Friedman, *The Shakespearean Ciphers Examined* (Cambridge, University Press, 1957). Referred to hereafter as Friedmans.

88

4. Marguerite

1. Dodd1, p. 84
2. Dodd1, p. 100.
3. Smedley, pp. 34–44.
4. Dawkins3, pp. 195–204.
5. *The Norton Facsimile First Folio of Shakespeare* (New York, W.W. Norton & Co., 2nd edition, 1996).

5. The Initiation

1. Christopher Knight and Robert Lomas, *The Hiram Key* (Boston, Element Books, 1998), pp. 330–333.
2. *ibid.*
3. Robert A. Monroe, *Ultimate Journey* (New York, Doubleday, 1994).
4. Kyriacos C. Markides, *Fire in the Heart; Healers, Sages and Mystics* (New York, Paragon House, 1990).
5. Sylvia Brown, *The Other Side and Back* (New York, Signet, 2000).
6. Elizabeth Kübler-Ross, *On Death and Dying* (New York, Simon and Schuster, 1997).

6. Abandoned

1. Fuller, p. 122.
2. Dodd1, p. 92.
3. Smedley, pp. 46–50.
4. Dawkins1, p. 58.
5. Francis Bacon, *Sylva Sylvarum: A Natural History in Ten Centuries* (London, 1628).
6. Paul Foster Case, *The True and Invisible Rosicrucian Order* (York Beach, Maine, Samuel Weiser, Inc., 1985).
7. Frances A. Yates, *The Rosicrucian Enlightenment* (London, Routledge and Kegan Paul, 1972).

7. The Suit

1. Dawkins3, pp. 266–268.
2. Francisci Baconi, *De Dignitate & Augmentis Scientarium* (London, 1623).
3. Mather Walker, *Edmund Spenser; The Man on the Stair* (Internet publication, www.sirbacon.org 2000).
4. *The Complete Works of William Shakespeare* (New York, Nelson Doubleday, 1966), pp. 1092–1113.
5. vK, p. 94.

6. vK, p. 76.
7. vK, p. 62.
8. Dodd1, p. 154.
9. Dodd1, p. 124.

8. The Rise of Essex

1. vK, p. 63.
2. Finn Leary, *Are There Ciphers in Shakespeare?* (Internet publication, www.att.net/˜tleary/home.htm 1993).
3. Nicholas Rowe, *The Life and Times of William Shakespeare* (London, 1709), Introduction.
4. Fuller, p. 125.
5. George Greenwood, *The Shakespeare Problem Restated* (London, John Lane Company, 1908). Referred to hereafter as Greenwood.
6. From Devereux's, *Lives of the Earls of Essex* according to Dodd1, p. 228.

9. Bacon Meets Shakesper

1. Dodd1, p. 187.
2. Smedley, p. 23.
3. Mark Alexander, *The Complete Shakspere/Shakespeare Documentary Evidence Chronologically Arranged* (Internet publication home.earthlink. net).
4. Robert Greene, *Groatsworth of Wit* (London, December, 1592).
5. Diana Price, *Shakespeare's Unorthodox Biography* (Westport, CT, Greenwood Press, 2001).
6. David L. Roper; see www.dlroper.shakespeareans.com

10. Gathering Clouds

1. W. Hepworth Dixon, *The Story of Lord Bacon's Life* (London, 1862), p. 62. Referred to hereafter as Dixon.
2. Mather Walker, *Resurrecting Marley* (Internet publication www.sirbacon. org/mmarley.htm November, 2000), p. 20.
3. Robert M. Theobald, *Shakespeare Studies in Baconian Light* (London, John Howard, 1901).
4. John Mitchell, *Who Wrote Shakespeare?* (Thames and Hudson, 1996).
5. See 2 above, p. 22.
6. Dodd1, p. 213.
7. James Spedding, *The Letters and Life of Francis Bacon*, volumes viii–xiv (London, 1861–74). Referred to hereafter as Spedding.
8. Francis Bacon, *A Device for the Gray's Inn Revels*, in Brian Vickers, ed. *Francis Bacon; A Critical Edition of the Major Works* (Oxford University Press, 1996).

9. Dodd1, p. 255.
10. Peter Dawkins, *Francis Bacon's Life; Brief Historical Sketch* (Internet publication, www.frbt.org).
11. Diana Price, *What's in a Name? Shakespeare, Shake-scene and the Clayton loan* (Internet article. See www.jmucci.com/ER/articles/price. htm).
12. Nicholas Rowe, *The Life and Times of William Shakespeare* (London, 1709), Introduction.
13. Mark Alexander, *The Complete Shakspere/Shakespeare Documentary Evidence Chronologically Arranged* (Internet publication home.earthlink. net). This is a comprehensive list of every known reference to Will Shaksper.
14. See ref. 11.
15. Fuller, p. 236.
16. Greenwood.
17. Charlton Ogburn, 'The Man Who Shakespeare Was Not (and Who He Was)', *Harvard Magazine* (November, 1974).
18. E.K. Chambers, *William Shakespeare – A Study of Facts and Problems* (Clarendon Press, Oxford, 1930).
19. D. Mallet, *The Life of Francis Bacon* (St Clements Church, 1665).
20. See 2 above, p. 21.
21. E.A. Abbott, *Francis Bacon; An Account of his Life and Works* (1885).
22. Irvin Leigh Matus, *Shakespeare In Fact* (New York, Continuum, 1999), p. 92.

11. Treachery

1. '*Francis Bacon, His Apologie In Certain Imputations Concerning the Late Earl of Essex*' (an open letter to the Earl of Devonshire, 1601). See, for example http://fly.hiway.net Referred to in the following as *Apologie*.
2. Mathews, p. 38.
3. Fuller, p. 151.
4. *Apologie*, p. 6.
5. *Apologie*, p. 7.
6. John Hayward, *The First Part of the Life and Raigne of King Henrie IIII Extending to the End of the First Yeare of his Raigne* (London, 1599).
7. *Apologie*, p. 9.
8. Francis Bacon, *Apophthegms* (London, 1625), number 58. *See also* reference 1 above, p. 7.
9. Fuller, p. 157.
10. Martin Pares, 'The Northumberland Transcript', *Baconiana* (March, 1960).
11. Robert Theobald, *Shakespeare Studies in Baconian Light* (XXX, 1901).
12. vK, p. 101.

13. Edward D. Johnson, *The Shakspere Illusion*. 3rd revised edition (London, Mitre Press, 1965).
14. Constance Pott, *The Promus of Formularies and Elegancies; Private Notes circa 1594, by Francis Bacon* (Boston, Houghton, Mifflin & Co., 1883).
15. Fuller, pp. 80–96.
16. Mather Walker, *The Evidence of Bacon's Mind in Shakespeare* (Internet publication, www.sirbacon.org), p. 27.

12. The Ring

1. Dodd1, p. 283.
2. Thomas Babington Macaulay, 'Francis Bacon', *Edinburgh Review* (July 1837).
3. Nieves Mathews, *Francis Bacon: The History of a Character Assassination* (Yale University Press, 1996), p. 45. Referred to hereafter as Mathews.
4. *The Arraignment, Trial and Condemnation of Robert Earl of Essex and Henry Earl of Southampton* (London, Thos. Basset, Sam. Heyrick, and Matth. Gillyflower, 1679). See www.renaissance.dm.net
5. Dodd1, p. 301.
6. Francis Osborne, *Historical Memoires on the Reigns of Queen Elizabeth and King James* (London, 1658), according to Dodd1, p. 301.
7. Dodd1, p. 302.
8. Dodd2, p. 80.
9. Dodd1, p. 309. See *Liverpool Daily Post*, July 28, 1930.
10. Dodd2, p. 81.
11. Dodd1, p. 312.

13. King James

1. Mathews, p. 43.
2. Nieves Mathews refers to (i) Menna Prestwich, *Cranfield, Politics and Profits under the Early Stuarts, The Career of Lionel Cranfield, Earl of Middlesex* (Oxford, 1966) and (ii) Joel Hurstfield, *The Queen's Wards* (London, 1958). Referred to hereafter as Hurstfield.
3. See www.sirbacon.org/newsletter1 also *London Sunday Dispatch*, Oct. 23, 1938.
4. Francis Bacon, *The New Atlantis* (London, 1627).
5. Dodd1, p. 376.
6. J.C. Bucknill, *The Mad Folk of Shakespeare* (1867).
7. Mark Alexander, 'Shakespeare's Bad Law' (Shakespeare Oxford Newsletter, winter 2000).
8. Greenwood.
9. Smedley, p. 154.
10. Dodd1, pp. 408–409.

11. Dodd1, p. 412.

14. Rising Star

1. Dodd1, pp. 420–421.
2. Gustavus S. Paine, *The Men Behind the King James Version* (Grand Rapids, Michigan, Baker Book House, 1959).
3. Fuller, p. 249.
4. Smedley, pp. 125–130.
5. William Strachey, *Historie of Traveile into Virginia Britannia* (London, 1625).
6. Penn Leary, *The Second Cryptographic Shakespeare* (Internet document: http://home.att.net/~mleary/pennl4.htm).
7. See, for example: Dave Kathman, *Dating The Tempest* (Internet publication; www.clark.net/pub/tross/ws/tempest.html).
8. John Aubrey, *Brief Lives* (London, 1679).
9. Frances A. Yates, *The Rosicrucian Enlightenment* (Ark, Reading, 1972).
10. Yates, p. 6.
11. Paul Foster Case, *The True and Invisible Rosicrucian Order* (York Beach ME, Samuel Weiser, 1992), pp. 3–4.
12. *Fama Fraternitatis*, anonymous, with a preface excerpted from *Universal and General Reformation of the Whole Wide World* by Trajano Boccalini (German; Kassel, Wilhelm Wessel, 1614).
13. *Confessio Fraternitatis*, anonymous, with a preface *A Brief Consideration of the more Secret Philosophy* by Philip à Gabella, a student of Philosophy (Latin; Kassel, Wilhelm Wessel, 1615).
14. Johann Valentin Andreae, *The Chemical Wedding of Christian Rosenkreutz; Anno 1459* (German; Strassburg, Lazarus Zetzner, 1616).
15. Peter Dawkins, *Bacon, Shakespeare and Fra. Christian Rose Cross* (London, Francis Bacon Research Trust, 1989), p. 5, with reference to the following reference number 16.
16. Robert Burton, *Anatomy of Melancholy* (London, 1621).
17. Francis Meres, *Palladis Tamia* (London, 1598).

15. The Fall

1. Harvey Wheeler, *The Semiosis of Francis Bacon's Scientific Empiricism* (Internet publication, see www.constitution.org/hwheeler 2001).
2. Peter Pesic, 'Wrestling with Proteus: Francis Bacon and the "Torture" of Nature', *Isis* (Volume 90, Number 1, March 1999).
3. Alan Soble, 'In Defense of Bacon', *Philosophy of the Social Sciences* (Vol. 25, June 1, 1995), p. 192.
4. Mathews, p. 131.
5. Dodd1, p. 524.
6. Mathews, p. 190.

7. Fuller, p. 284.
8. Fuller, p. 279.
9. Dixon, pp. 429–430.
10. Samuel R. Gardiner, *History of England from the Accession of James I to the outbreak of the Civil War, 1603–1642, volumes ii to iv, 1863–1869*, as referred to by Mathews, pp. 170–171.
11. Mathews, p. 430.
12. Hurstfield, p. 182.
13. Spedding, xiv, p. 277.

16. The Final Curtain

1. Bacon's full statement and his subsequent detailed comments can be found on www.british-history.ac.uk under *Journal of the House of Lords*, vol. 3, April 24, 1621 and April 30, 1621.
2. Mathews, p. 173.
3. Mathews, p. 176.
4. Dodd1, p. 528.
5. vK, p. 115.
6. vK, p. 115.
7. Fuller, p. 295.
8. Edwin Reed, *Francis Bacon; Our Shakespeare* (Boston, Charles E. Goodspeed, 1902). For others, see previous references.
9. Orville W. Owen, M.D., *The Medicine in Shakespeare* (See www.sirbacon. org/owencirculation.htm).
10. Reed, p. 9.
11. Reed, p. 11.
12. Reed, p. 25.
13. Reed, p. 32.
14. Fuller, p. 310.
15. Peter Dickson, *Henry Peacham and the First Folio of 1623* (Internet publication, www.elizreview.com/articles/peacham.htm), p. 3.
16. Smedley, pp. 181–182.
17. William Rawley, ed., *Manes Verulamiani* (London, John Haviland, 1626).
18. Steven Sora, *The Lost Treasure of the Knights Templar; Solving the Oak Island Mystery* (Rochester, Vermont, Destiny Books, 1999).
19. Mark Finnan, *Oak Island Secrets* (Halifax, Nova Scotia, Formac Publishing, 1997).
20. *Sylva Sylvarum*, p. 7.

17. Return to Parnassus

1. Kyriacos Markides, *Fire in the Heart* (London, Penguin Group, 1990).
2. Elizabeth Kübler-Ross, *On Death and Dying* (London, Tavistock Publications, 1970).

3. Raymond A. Moody, *Reflections on Life After Life* (Stackpole Books, Pennsylvania, 1977).

18. Concluding Comments

1. N.B. Cockburn, *The Bacon Shakespeare Question; The Baconian theory made sane* (London, N.B. Cockburn, 1998).
2. Fuller, pp. 229–240.
3. Penn Leary, *Are There Ciphers in Shakespeare?* (Internet publication; home.att.net/..tleary), and *The Second Cryptographic Shakespeare* (home.att.net/..mleary).
4. Mather Walker, *The Secret of the Shakespeare Plays* (Internet publication; www.sirbacon.org).
5. T.D. Bokenham, *A Brief History of the Bacon-Shakespeare Controversy* (The Francis Bacon Trust Publications, 1982).
6. Kenneth R. Patton, *Setting the Record Straight* (Internet publication; www.sirbacon.org).
7. Friedmans, p. 112.
8. Jerome Harner, *Why I'm not an Oxfordian; Bacon versus de Vere* (Internet publication, www.sirbacon.org, 2001).